# TABLE OF CONTENTS

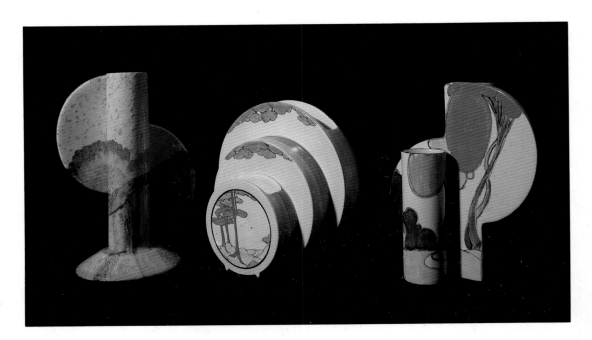

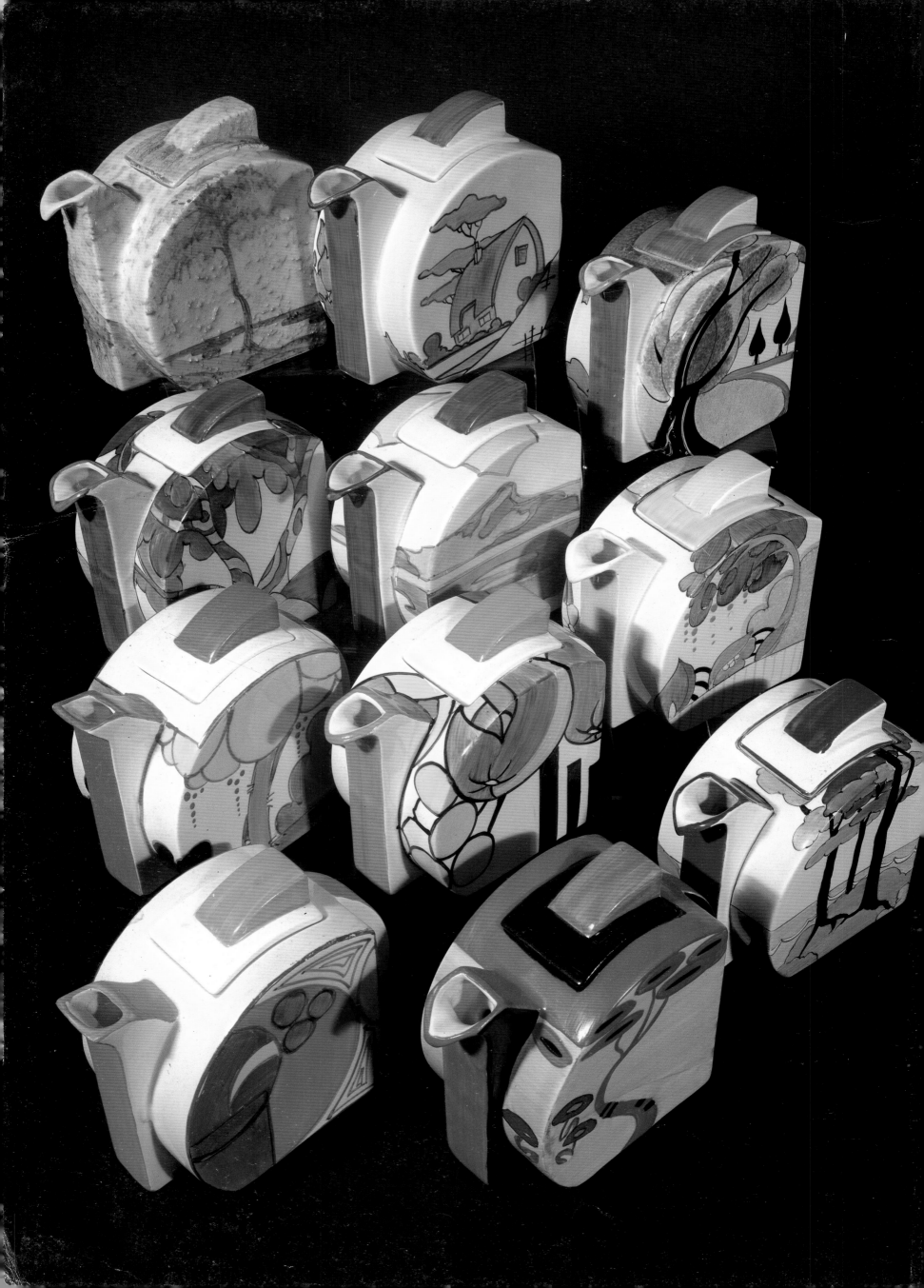

# G...f

# THE ... FAIR

## by Leonard Griffin and Louis K. and Susan Pear Meisel

### With Photography by Murray Alcosser

## Thames and Hudson

**Front cover:**
The SUNRAY design on a fifteen-inch-high shape 14 vase, a 186 vase, and a CONICAL teapot. These pieces date from late 1929 or 1930.

**Page 1:**
A fifteen-inch high hexagonal vase, shape number 37, decorated in the blue colorway of AUTUMN. The vase shape was introduced in the 1920s; this piece dates from 1931.

**Page 2:**
Sugar sifters: a CONICAL shape (489) in the BLUE CHINTZ pattern, an old Newport shape with chrome top, and a BON JOUR in GREEN ERIN.

**Page 3, above:**
Three of the vase shapes Clarice produced to complement her BIZARRE designs. A 366 vase in the RUDYARD pattern, a FERN pot shape 421 in RED ROOFS, and a STAMFORD shape vase 460 in AUTUMN BLUE. These shapes were produced only in small quantities but were in production from 1929 to approximately 1934. The two larger vases are six inches high. Collections of Mrs. Betty Scott and Leonard Griffin.

**Page 3, below:**
Three unusual vases produced in the early 1930s: on the left a FLOWER TUBE shape 464 decorated in PATINA "COUNTRY." The shape first appeared in 1931. The six-inch-high TRIPLE BON JOUR vase in the middle first appeared in 1934. This example is decorated in CORAL FIRS. On the right is shape 465, a DOUBLE FLOWER TUBE (the taller tube is concealed) decorated in ORANGE AUTUMN. The shape dates from 1931. Collections of Mrs. Betty Scott and Leonard Griffin.

**Page 4:**
A collection of STAMFORD teapots. Top row: PATINA "TREE," PINK ROOF COTTAGE, and MAY AVENUE; second row: RUDYARD, GIBRALTAR, and MOONLIGHT; third row: SUMMERHOUSE, APPLE, and BLUE FIRS; bottom row: MELON and APPLIQUE "RED TREE." The MELON and SUMMERHOUSE examples have the earlier straight lip on the spout, which was adapted to improve pouring. Collections of Leonard Griffin and David and Pauline Latham.

**Page 5:**
A selection of CONICAL sugar sifters, shape 489. Top row: SECRETS, HOUSE AND BRIDGE, BROOKFIELDS, RED ROOFS; second row: CORAL FIRS, FARMHOUSE, PASTEL AUTUMN; third row: RUDYARD, LIMBERLOST, CAFE-AU-LAIT AUTUMN; bottom row: BLUE CHINTZ, ORANGE ERIN, MELON. Collections of David and Pauline Latham and Leonard Griffin.

**Page 6:**
Single- and double-handled LOTUS jugs. Top row: APPLIQUE AVIGNON, WINDBELLS, SOLITUDE; second row: APPLIQUE LUGANO, SUNRAY, BLUE JAPAN; third row: FARMHOUSE, HONOLULU, SUMMERHOUSE; bottom row: BLUE AUTUMN, PASTEL AUTUMN, AUTUMN variant. All twelve inches high.

**Page 7, above:**
The LOTUS jug (also referred to in the sales literature as an ISIS jug) in its four sizes: six-inch RHODANTHE (1934), eight-inch PINE GROVE (1935), ten-inch BUTTERFLY (1930), and twelve-inch DELECIA CITRUS (1932). Generally the twelve-inch size was called LOTUS and the ten-inch version ISIS.

**Page 7, below:**
Several variations of the very rare CLOUVRE design: CLOUVRE TULIP on a twelve-inch LOTUS jug and a 269 vase, and CLOUVRE MARIGOLD on a pair of 391 candlesticks and a shape 200 vase.

**Page 8:**
The SLICED CIRCLE design on a fifteen-inch shape 14 vase. Produced 1929 or 1930.

**Page 9, clockwise from upper left:**
A CONICAL cookie jar, shape number 402, in the MOONLIGHT design; a twelve-inch vase, shape number 779, in the STILE AND TREES design, 1937; a STAMFORD cookie jar decorated in CHINTZ ORANGE, 1932; an old Newport shape vase in the FANTASQUE LILY design, 1929.

**Back cover:**
An extremely fine example of the PERSIAN design on a two-handled LOTUS jug, 1930.

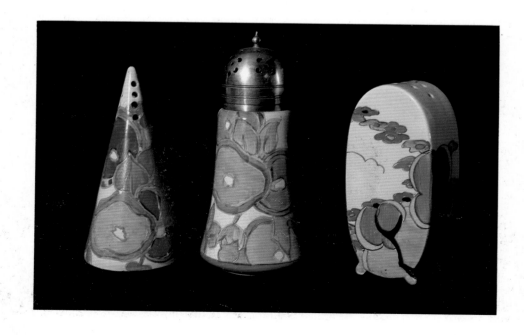

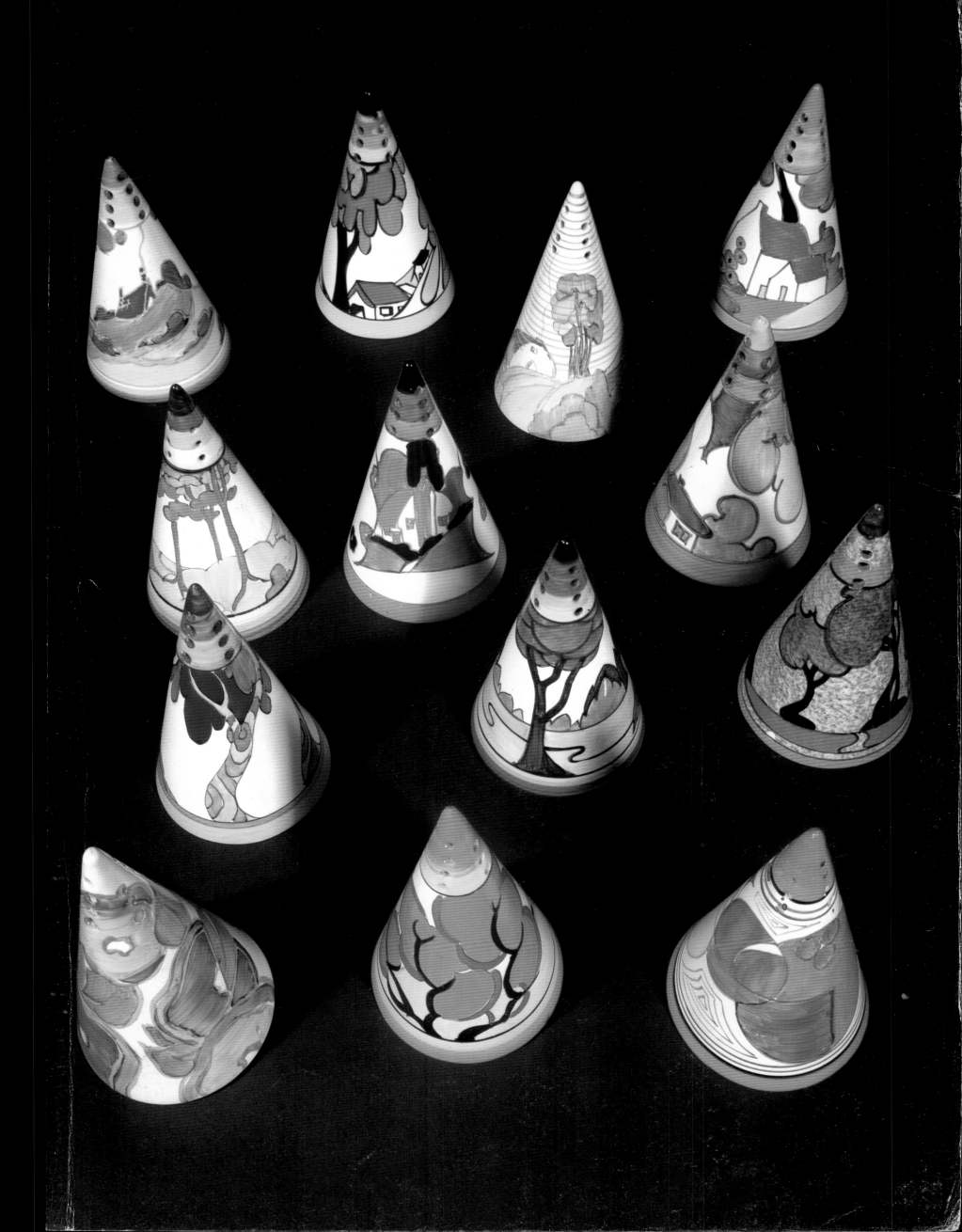

## Preface

During a trip to Minneapolis in 1971 to visit the studios of two artists I was considering representing at my gallery, I happened to stop at The Minneapolis Institute of Arts. The exhibit at the time was an extraordinarily broad survey entitled "The World of Art Deco," which included examples of the art and design of this 1920s period. Bevis Hillier prepared a catalogue for this exhibition. The exhibition was a landmark in the resurgence of Clarice Cliff pottery to the United States as true art pottery and as collectible antiques. It contained over fifty pieces of work by Clarice Cliff, and it was my introduction to her work and the beginning of a series of events that led to the publication of this book.

I had been collecting various objects since I turned ten in 1952. I had been in hundreds of antique shops but had never seen or noticed anything like the works of Cliff on display in Minneapolis. One year later, during a visit to the Morgan Gallery in Kansas City, I saw my first private collection of *Bizarre* pottery. Jim "Poppa" Morgan, a former TWA pilot with a great eye who spent his off hours searching all over the world for interesting objects, assembled the collection. Shortly thereafter, Arthur Cohen, an astute and visionary collector, showed me his collection of Cliff, which included some of the best works I had yet seen.

By 1978, Arthur, knowing my penchant for fanatical collection, and my wife, Susan, who has a terrific eye on a purely aesthetic level, teamed up to get me involved in yet another collection. I sold a painting from my Abstract Expressionist collection and bought our first seven pieces of Clarice Cliff from Joia, to my knowledge the first shop in New York to actively show Cliff. Joia had mostly acquired their pieces from Noel Tovey in London, at L'Odeon.

My conscious goal in all my collecting is to assemble a group of objects that will ultimately, because of their careful selection, become worthy of study and of scholarly value to others than myself. As a collector, I wish to learn, teach, share, and publish; hence this book.

Once we made the commitment nothing could stop us. Susan placed advertisements in classified sections of newspapers in likely counties and cities, and about a dozen dealers offered us pieces. The single most important dealers to us by far, however, were Ernie and Shirley Mellet in London. Before we began frequent trips to London, and before Sotheby's and Christie's began auctioning Cliff, the Mellets searched all of Britain and came up with hundreds of incredible items for us. Our collection is at least 50 percent due to their efforts, and without them I do not know if we could have done any of this.

By the time Christie's ran its now famous Clarice Cliff auction in June 1983, we had the largest collection in the United States and perhaps in the world. For this auction I flew to London, and in somewhat of a publicity stunt, bought forty of the forty-two most important works for over half the value of the sale. That summer there was a four-column article by Rita Reif in *The New York Times* about Clarice Cliff and the auction. This enormous publicity led to many more articles and interviews.

Soon many of the collector-dealers who showed my contemporary artists wanted to introduce Clarice Cliff in their cities. Instead of a piece or two just turning up in antique shops, Cliff was instead introduced in art galleries in beautiful exhibitions. Lori Kaufman in Chicago, John Berggruen in California, and the Byer Museum of the Arts in Evanston, Illinois, the first museum to do a Cliff exhibition, are just a few of the galleries that started the interest rolling. We supplied all the work for these events.

In 1982 the curator of twentieth-century design at The Metropolitan Museum of Art in New York requested and received for their collections six items from our personal collection. These pieces have been on view a great amount of time, winning new admirers and avid collectors.

In 1984 I asked Leonard Griffin to collaborate with me to produce this book. Len is the world's leading expert on the life and work of Clarice Cliff.

I asked Murray Alcosser, one of the world's leading still life photographers, to photograph our collection to illustrate this book. The results are evident.

Arthur Cohen got us started. Ernie Mellet worked with us for years helping us to assemble our collection. Len Griffin has seemingly documented every minute and idea in the life of Clarice Cliff. Paul Gottlieb, the president and publisher of Abrams, immediately understood and embraced the beauty and importance of Clarice Cliff and agreed to publish this book. This book, with its massive amount of information, will be a guide for all present and future collectors, dealers, museums, and scholars.

For the reader who wishes to see and learn more and or acquire works by Clarice Cliff, the books and catalogues listed in the Bibliography will be helpful. The following stores and dealers can also be helpful with information and acquisitions: In London, L'Odeon, 175 Fulman Road; several shops in Chenil Galleries Arcade on Kings Road; and several shops in Antiquarius Arcade, 135 Kings Road. In New York, Joia, Second Avenue at Sixtieth Street; Primavera, 808 Madison Avenue; and Meisel Primavera, 133 Prince Street in SoHo.

Louis K. Meisel

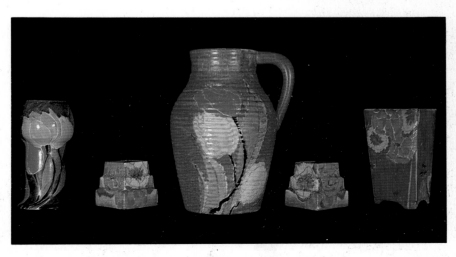

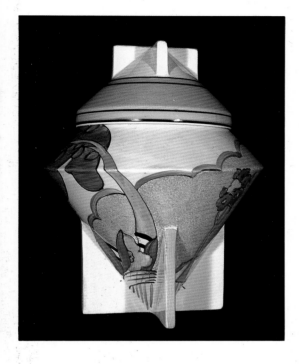

# Introduction
## by Leonard Griffin

Few can resist a rags to riches success story. And if success comes not through some happy accident but through hard work, relentless dedication, and the flowering of a remarkable talent, then the story becomes even more appealing. Clarice Cliff lived such a story: a working-class girl of seemingly limited prospects, she became, in the opinion of many, the most important ceramic designer of her generation. The development of her art, in its sheer magnitude and diversity, might be considered even more fascinating than the story of her life if the two were not inextricably interwoven.

One purpose of this volume is to tell of her life and art. In the course of gathering material for this book, a process that involved interviewing dozens of the people with whom Clarice worked, talking with countless collectors of the Art Deco period, and reviewing the archives of her collections, the story behind her art—the very human motivating factors—emerged. It is the story of the forces that prompted individual designs, the development of production processes, the handling of marketing problems, the indispensable contribution of the talented young artists who worked with Clarice, and the relationship she had with her employer.

This book also contains a comprehensive guide to the names and dates of Clarice's vast range of designs and shapes and is intended as a practical reference for collectors. The constantly rising value of her ware and its seemingly endless variety demands such a source. While collectors will undoubtedly form their own opinions of her work, they will nevertheless find value in the general consensus of what is merely very good, what is spectacular, and what deserves to be forgotten.

The most important function this volume might fulfill, however, is to help us to understand and appreciate the uniqueness of Clarice's art. She appropriately named her work *Bizarre*, and the young artists who decorated her pottery proudly called themselves the *Bizarre* girls. What is it about her designs that make them so special? Why is Clarice's work impossible to ignore, eliciting a full range of response from hate to love? Why is it that pottery produced in a factory rather than a studio and designed as primarily functional rather than decorative elicits such emotion that it has become among the most collectible of all the ceramics produced in this century? It is not possible to answer such questions with mere words and illustrations. The answer lies within each individual who experiences her art in the original. It is hoped that readers will see this volume, first and foremost, as a guide to that experiencing process.

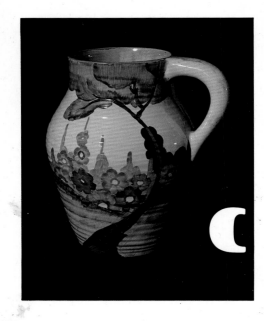

## Chapter One
### 1899 to 1920

larice Cliff was born in January of 1899 in Tunstall, in the county of Staffordshire, Britain's premier pottery-producing region. Her birthplace was studded with hundreds of factories churning out earthenware and rough-cast figures painted in bright Staffordshire ceramic colors. Such goods had been produced continuously in the region since the 1720s, and Clarice's ancestors had lived in Staffordshire since 1725.

Clarice, however, did not descend from a distinguished line of potters; her father was an iron molder, and her mother, Ann, with eight children to care for, had no time to work outside the home. Clarice was not part of an advantaged family that could nurture her interest in the arts. To the casual observer she was just an average, working-class child in a factory town of seemingly endless streets of terraced houses, with their outside toilets, gas lighting, and Friday night baths in the kitchen. While no one in town went hungry, few had money to spare, and it was expected that all members of the large families would work at the earliest opportunity to supplement the household income.

Clarice's early childhood was unremarkable, with little to suggest that she alone among her family would one day leave the world of terraced houses to carve out a brilliant career. In one small way, however, Clarice's early years did differ from those of her siblings. Upon reaching school age, she was not sent to the same school as the other children in her family. This was not for educational reasons but simply so that she could deliver a lunch box to a friend of the family before school each day. The lack of brothers and sisters to help her through the tribulations that all young children encounter at school may have helped to instill in Clarice the spirit of independence later reflected in her art.

Academically Clarice was of average ability; there is little worth noting about her years at the High Street Elementary School except that she showed an interest in drawing. Her artistic bent was only barely nurtured, however, in the thirty minutes allotted to the subject each week. Another outlet for her art interests developed when, at the age of ten, she transferred to the Summerbank Road School to finish her education. There, Clarice took every opportunity to make clay models. And her interest in working at a "pot bank," as the local factories were called, was stimulated when, often, after school, she visited her aunt who was in charge of the decorating shop at Alfred Meakin's factory in Tunstall. Clarice went to the shop frequently, for she was fascinated by the speed with which the decorators painted the ware, and when they tired of her questions, they gave her a lump of clay to model.

Above left:
The FRAGRANCE design on an eight-inch jug with experimental overpainting. 1935.

Above right:
The ORANGE ERIN design on an ISIS shape vase. 1934.

Opposite:
Single-handled LOTUS jugs. Top row: three early abstract designs, in the middle SLICED FRUIT; second row: "FRUIT BURST," LATONA DAHLIA, "RED FLOWER," UMBRELLAS AND RAIN; third row: MELON variant, GARDENIA, MELON; fourth row: DELECIA CITRUS, ANEMONE, "BLUE DAISY," CANTERBURY BELLS. All twelve inches high.

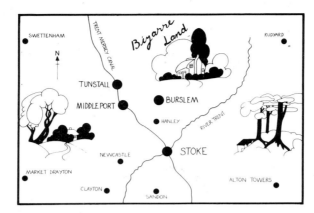

An idealized map placing "BIZARRE Land" in the context of the other pottery-producing towns in the Stoke-on-Trent area. Distances between towns are not to scale.

Childhood was a very brief phase in the Potteries; few youngsters had the opportunity to continue their formal education beyond the age of thirteen. Clarice was no exception, and in 1912 she joined the Tunstall earthenware manufacturing firm of Lingard, Webster and Company as an apprentice in the enameling trade, where she was trained in the art of painting freehand onto pottery. She was paid one shilling for a five-and-a-half-day work week, giving most of her earnings to her mother and using the little that was left to buy the "pencils" and palette knives essential to her trade.

Although her apprenticeship in the enameling trade was meant to last seven years, in 1915 Clarice joined the Tunstall firm of Hollinshead and Kirkham as an apprentice in lithography. Her parents felt that she should continue with her hand-painting and clay-modeling, however, and so paid for her to attend evening classes at the Tunstall School of Art.

Only one year later, in 1916, an even better opportunity appeared. Because most of the young men were off fighting in World War I, staff shortages existed at the Potteries. The need for additional workers was especially great at the A. J. Wilkinson earthenware factory in the town of Middleport. The firm's new directors, Colley and Guy Shorter, were greatly increasing sales. When Clarice heard of a job opening in the decorating department at Wilkinson's, she eagerly applied. Wilkinson's was a larger firm than Hollinshead and Kirkham, and Clarice knew she would have much better prospects there. Clarice's decision would prove to be the most important of her career.

On the first day at her new job, Clarice arrived without an apron, although each girl was expected to provide her own. Jack Walker, the decorating manager at Wilkinson's and Colley Shorter's brother-in-law, recognizing that Clarice was a talented girl from a poor family, took her under his wing. He made sure that an apron was found for her and that she was settled into the lithography department. He found her quite likable and subsequently took a close interest in her work both at the factory and in evening art classes.

Clarice, in turn, made the most of her opportunity at Wilkinson's. She often spent her lunch breaks wandering about the factory's various departments, learning about kilns, glazing, and other technical processes. At other times she would spend her breaks modeling crude figures and animals from lumps of clay.

Clarice became so involved with her work and her art classes that her social life grew quite limited and confined mainly to weekends. She showed little interest in the dances that her sisters and other girls of the Potteries regularly attended. Like most in the Potteries at that time, however, Clarice was quite religious, and she regularly attended Christ Church in Tunstall. From 1917 on she taught Sunday school classes there, and this, plus the services at the church, took up most of her weekends. What little time remained she spent making her own clothes so that she would have a choice of dresses for her "Sunday best."

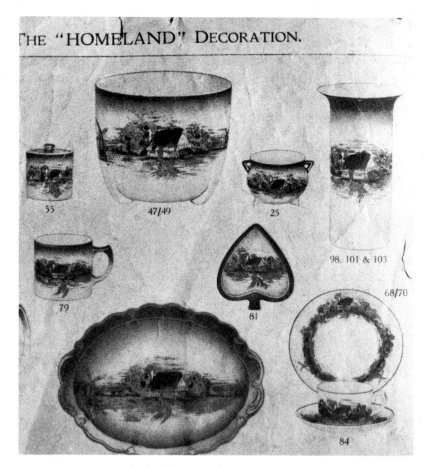

A portion of a 1924 sales sheet for the Newport Pottery's
HOMELAND ware. The sales sheet was produced
lithographically.

Part of A. J. Wilkinson's Pottery along the Trent Mersey
Canal, as it appeared in the 1920s. In the background
can be seen the Pottery's bottle-kilns.

A teaset for four in the TREES AND HOUSE design, with
a mixed shaped set, consisting of a STAMFORD teapot,
CONICAL milk jug, cups, and saucers, and a FERN HEATH
shape sugar bowl. The LOTUS jug in the same design is
twelve inches high. 1930 or 1931.

When World War I ended in 1918, Clarice became
even more absorbed in her work. There was an increasing demand for inexpensive, functional earthenware,
much of it barely changed from what had been produced in the region for more than two centuries. Colley
and Guy Shorter responded to this demand by increasing their factory's output, and Wilkinson's soon became one of the most important in the area. Many
talented artists and tradesmen had lost their lives in
the war. This opening was to present a golden opportunity for Clarice, but she did not realize it at the time, as
the output of Wilkinson's was quite pedestrian.

Examples of the work produced during this time include black prints of Buckingham Palace and Windsor
Castle that were put on the ware. Orange luster would
then be sprayed on, cleaned off, and then enamel colors
would be applied. Simpler designs consisted of a lithograph around the top of a vase, with bright lilac or yellow airbrushed around the rest of it. The lithographs
were not created at Wilkinson's; rather, they were
mass-produced rolls purchased commercially. They
came in narrow widths that fit easily around the top of
any vase or jug. The required length would be cut from
the roll by the lithographer and then fitted on the ware.

Some of the shapes used to produce this ware were
numbers 14, 16, 20, and the series numbered 120 to
220. Clarice did not personally create these shapes, for
she was not yet entrusted with the responsibility of
conceiving new shapes and designs. They are, however, representative of those she decorated during her
early years at Wilkinson's.

As the decade closed, Clarice was just a lithographer
helping to turn out mass-produced designs. She was
eager to improve herself but not really sure how she
was going to do it.

A selection of landscape designs. Top row: HOUSE AND
BRIDGE, ORANGE ROOF COTTAGE, and DEVON; second
row: RED ROOFS and POPLAR; third row: BRIDGEWATER
ORANGE, MAY AVENUE on a thirteen-inch charger, and
ORANGE HOUSE; fourth row: DOUBLE BON JOUR shape
candlestick in BRIDGEWATER GREEN and 378 vase in
SECRETS; bottom row: GREEN HOUSE on a 371 vase,
CAFE-AU-LAIT AUTUMN on a shape 14 vase, and KEW on a
CONICAL jug. Collections of David and Pauline Latham
and Leonard Griffin.

The building that housed the BIZARRE shop, the CROCUS
shop, and the packing room, pictured in 1985.

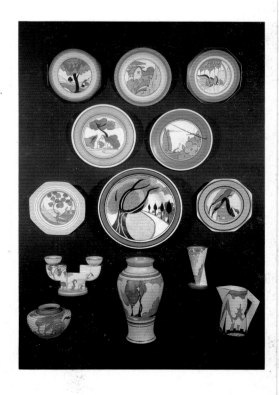

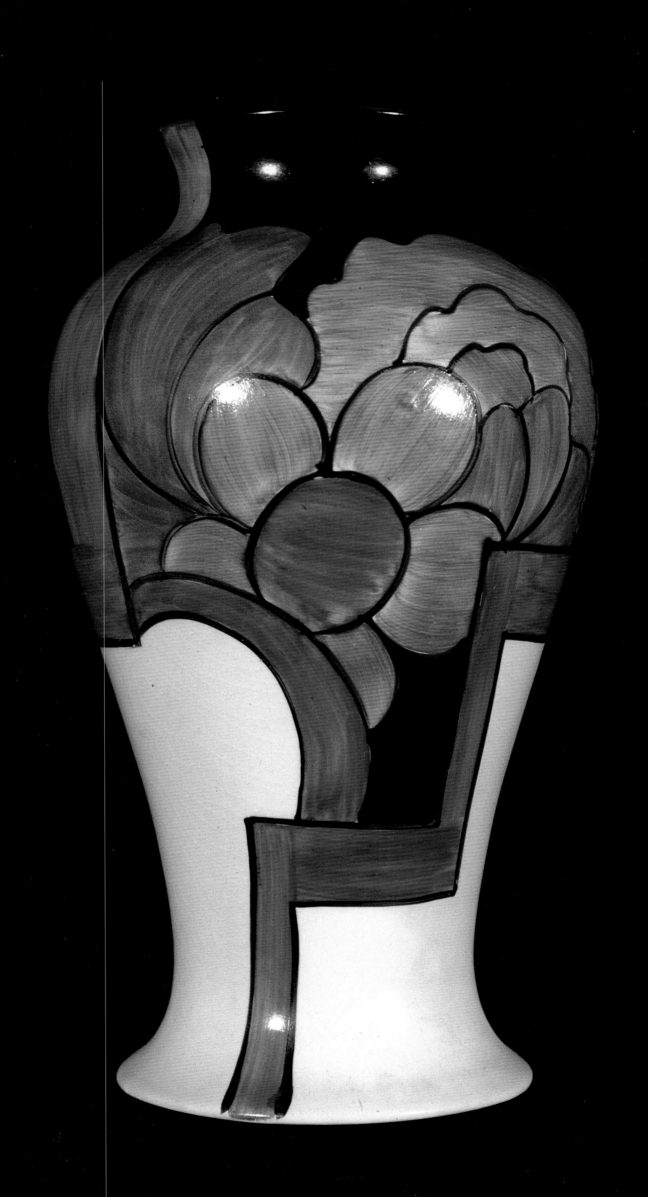

## Chapter Two
## 1920 to 1927

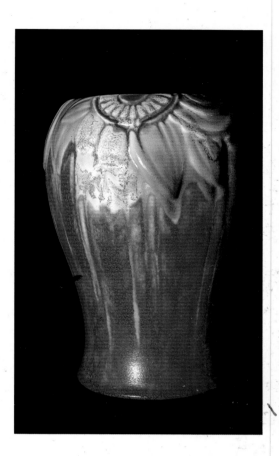

n 1920 Clarice got a lucky break. After work one evening, Jack Walker noticed her hand-painting a piece of ware. He realized she had the potential to do more than just copy other people's designs and discussed this with Colley Shorter. Together the two decided to give her a chance to develop her talent. Clarice was moved from the general decorating shop to work alongside Wilkinson's two top designers, John Butler and Fred Ridgeway.

Butler and Ridgeway worked in a studio separate from the main production area and produced high-quality ware not at all typical of the output of the factory. Their work was carefully done and very expensive; it was intended to give the factory prestige to help sell the more everyday ware. Clarice herself acquired increased prestige just from being associated with them. She was also rewarded with an increase in pay.

More important than money and prestige was the greater opportunity for learning Clarice now had. For example, she helped John Butler to produce the distinctive *Tibetan* line that he had pioneered. The ware was covered in lustrous runnings in rich golds and purples, which were then finely outlined in gold, often with small abstract designs added to them. Clarice was entrusted to do some of the fine gold outlining. This ware was awarded a diploma of honor at a trade exhibition at Ghent.

Fred Ridgeway's designs were very much of the Victorian era—trees, streams, Chinese lanterns, waterfalls, and butterflies, all very finely executed. Unfortunately, Ridgeway took a personal dislike to Clarice and rarely spoke to her; their working relationship was nevertheless productive. The first reference in the Wilkinson's archives to Clarice alludes to her assisting Ridgeway with one of his elaborate Victorian designs, this one executed on a plaque. The reference is to pattern number 7309, which dates from February 1923, and includes the note "CC does the gold."

**Above left:**
The LIGHTNING design on a TANKARD shape coffeepot.
1929 or 1930.

**Above right:**
An old, embossed Newport Pottery shape vase decorated
in INSPIRATION glaze to make it saleable.

**Opposite:**
The LATONA DAHLIA design on a shape 14 vase, 1930.

A HAVRE shape bowl in the MAY AVENUE pattern, a 356 jardiniere in BROTH, and an old Newport shape bowl in PATINA COUNTRY.

The first known reference to Clarice Cliff, "gilt by C.C.," from the Wilkinson pattern books of February 1923.

In 1923 Clarice also helped decorate a line called *Oriflamme*. It was produced in the rich colors of the *Tibetan* ware but by an entirely different technique. The ware was covered in a swirling amorphous mass of gold and purple shades, probably done at least in part by airbrush. The effect was completely random, and no two pieces are identical. In the best examples the gold forms lightning-like patterns through the deep purple background.

The *Oriflamme* technique was actually achieved by a Mr. Eaton under John Butler's supervision. Little is known of Mr. Eaton: he worked only briefly at the factory, and when he left production of *Oriflamme* ceased. The better pieces of *Oriflamme* were also hand-painted with elaborate designs by Fred Ridgeway. Pattern number 7499 from the Wilkinson archives, dating from October 1923, is described in the pattern book as vase shape number 40, with *Oriflamme* by Mr. Eaton and a green and brown landscape painted by Mr. Ridgeway. Clarice was responsible for the gilding of such ware.

By 1924, Clarice first produced pieces with her name on them, while continuing to work on the *Oriflamme* and *Tibetan* line. Her major interest was still clay modeling, and she made small, highly detailed figures with heavily etched surfaces. She then painted them and put an impressed "Clarice C." mark on the side and a Wilkinson's mark on the base. Most of these figures are of Indians or Arabs and are very naively styled. They are quite rare, and it seems unlikely that they were ever produced to be sold. Probably they are pieces Clarice was asked to produce as part of her training.

In addition to her work at the factory, Clarice continued with her evening art classes; by this time she had transferred to the Burslem School of Art, attending classes two nights a week because she could not afford the tuition for full-time study.

In 1925, Clarice moved from her family home in Tunstall to take her own apartment over a hairdresser's shop in the town of Hanley. Her family was displeased with the move; it was not considered proper for a young, unmarried woman to live alone. Until this time there had been no hint of scandal in Clarice's life. What spare time she had was spent in church activities or practicing clay modeling. She still showed no interest in going dancing like the other girls her age and was never known to have a boyfriend, either at the factory or in Tunstall. Her simple life-style, however, was soon to come to an end.

That same year, Clarice ended her evening art classes. Meanwhile, Colley Shorter gave her career a considerable boost by providing her with a private studio right next to his office in the Newport Pottery, an adjacent facility just purchased by Wilkinson's. It was more than just a room; it also gave Clarice access to a photographic studio and darkroom. In these she taught herself to produce and print the factory's publicity pictures, which she continued to do right up until the success of *Bizarre* forced her to relinquish this part of her work.

Colley Shorter was a very busy man, what with the continuing expansion of Wilkinson's and the acquisition of the Newport Pottery; nevertheless he found time to be Clarice's most frequent visitor, spending more and more time behind the closed door of her studio. It is possible that Colley spent the long, secluded hours with Clarice simply giving advice and listening to her ideas. The appearance, however, was of activities considerably less innocent, for Clarice was a very attractive young woman. She had deep blue eyes and luxurious, long, black hair, and, with her considerable talent for making her own clothes, she was always very fashionably dressed. Colley, on the other hand, was seventeen years older than Clarice and had a wife and

The A. J. Wilkinson stand, featuring TIBETAN and ORIFLAMME ware, at a trade show in Philadelphia in 1926.

The Prospect Street entrance to Wilkinson's. At left is the bell tower, below that Dolly Cliff's shop, and at right the massive ovens and bottle kilns.

The entrance to Midwinter's, formerly the A. J. Wilkinson factory, in the 1980s.

two children. The daily liaisons between the wealthy employer and his protégée caused tongues to wag, but, as Colley's wife was chronically ill and somewhat of a recluse, it is probable that she at least never heard of any impropriety.

Clarice's friendly relations with the other girls at the factory ended with the spread of gossip about her and Colley. Her co-workers now treated her in a proper civil manner but kept their distance. They were careful never to talk about Clarice if Colley was within hearing range, and, with no job security whatsoever, they were especially careful of what they said in front of Clarice.

Jack Walker and Guy Shorter, Colley's brother, also distanced themselves from Clarice, speaking to her only when it was necessary for business purposes. Clarice was particularly hurt by Walker's remoteness because he had always supported her. Having been rebuffed by her old friends, Clarice could turn only to Colley Shorter with any confidence.

With Colley taking a decidedly personal interest in her career, Clarice's talents grew. In the spring of 1927 Colley decided to give her more formal training and sent her for a two-month course at London's Royal College of Art in Kensington, one of the top colleges in Britain. He even arranged to have the college's requirements for advance application and interview waived in Clarice's case. Wilkinson's paid for the course, an unusual circumstance because Colley Shorter was renowned for his stinginess.

At Royal College Clarice studied clay modeling of the head and figure, working from live models. She also took instruction in figure composition and life-drawing. On May 26, the last day of her studies, the registrar, Mr. Wellington, wrote to Colley: "I promised to give you some report of the work that she has done and the opinion we formed of her ability. There is little doubt that she has native ability. I consider that the figure she has just modeled shows a surprising advance on her work of two months ago, and if financial circumstances had not to be taken into account, but only the development of her talent considered, I should say, go on studying for two or three years."

Clarice's studies at Royal College were interrupted in late 1927 when, at Colley's expense, she took a trip to Paris. She spent her time there absorbing the work of French designers, buying art books, and visiting galleries. She returned to Wilkinson's brimming with ideas and excitedly discussed them with Colley. Fate played an important part in turning Clarice's ideas into reality, for while she was studying Colley had agreed, at the request of the British Pottery Manufacturers association, to take on trained apprentices from the Burslem School of Art the following summer. These young artists would later form the core of her decorating team.

But first she had to prove herself on a smaller scale. Clarice knew that with the purchase of the Newport Pottery, Wilkinson's had acquired thousands of pieces of ware in very dated shapes, and that many of the pieces had manufacturing defects. Clarice's idea was to cover the ware, faults and all, with bright colors in order to make them saleable. She asked to set up an experimental shop to put her ideas into practice. Colley assigned a talented fifteen-year-old apprentice, Gladys Scarlett, to work with her on the experiment.

As 1927 drew to a close they embarked on their experiment. Clarice showed Gladys how she wanted her to test the different methods of covering the ware in bright colors. The two did not talk much, but their suppressed excitement must have been great. Clarice was getting her big chance to prove her talents, and Gladys got her first step toward becoming a designer. It was crucial to both that their experiment be successful.

Above: ORIGINAL BIZARRE designs on three old Newport shapes: unknown, vase 187, and vase 186. 1928 or 1929.

# BIZARRE WARE

NEWPORT POTTERY
CO., LTD.

*Newport Pottery*
*B U R S L E M*
STAFFORDSHIRE, ENGLAND

SMEDLEY SERVICE.

1. Honey, No. 398.
2. Empire Teacup and Saucer.
3. Globe Teapot, 3 sizes.
4. Tankard Coffee Pot, 3 sizes.
5. Coffee Can and Saucer.
6. Candlestick, No. 331, 2" high.
7. Octagon Bowl, 3 sizes, 7", 8", 9".
8. Bowl, No. 147, 3 sizes, 7", 8", 9".
9. Octagon Bowl, 3 sizes, 7", 8", 9".
10. Elton Candlestick, 2 sizes, 8", 10".
11. "Eve" Bulb Box, 3".
12. Vase, No. 186, 3 sizes, 8¼", 7", 5½".
13. Vase, No. 205, size 5½".
14. Biscuit Jar, Hereford.
15. Ginger Jar, No. 6.
16. Dover Pot, 5 sizes, 5" to 8½".
17. Apple Honey.
18. Flower Holder, No. 537, size 4½".
19. Vase, No. 208, size 6".
20. Vase, No. 141, size 9".
21. Isis Vase, 2 handles, size 11½".
22. Vase, No. 120, size 10".
23. Vase, No. 269, size 5½".

**Left:**
A 1928 sales leaflet for what was to become known as ORIGINAL BIZARRE. This was the first advertising material produced for the new ware, and it appeared before Clarice had produced any new shapes: all the shapes shown are old Newport ones. Interestingly, number 17, listed as an ISIS vase, would have had "Lotus shape" impressed on its base. It is not known why the factory changed the name of this piece, but with so many examples marked LOTUS, this name is firmly established and is the one used throughout the book. ISIS is used for the vases of the same shape without the handles.

**Below:**
CAULDRON in the MELON design and an old Newport shape, PERTH jug, in AUTUMN RED.

**Bottom:**
Honey pots in the APPLE shape decorated in ORIGINAL BIZARRE pattern, DRUM shape in MELON, and 230 shape in SUMMERHOUSE.

The RAVEL pattern on an old Newport Pottery jug.

he senior staff at Wilkinson's were skeptical of Clarice's experiment. The salesmen were doubtful that her work would sell. Only Colley Shorter remained enthusiastic, and he was consistent in his encouragement and support of Clarice.

He saw potential in the bright geometric decorations with which Clarice and Gladys were covering the old Newport stock. He also liked the work Clarice was doing independently, for her modeling had developed greatly since the days when she had created crude figures of exotic peoples.

She had previously produced a figure of a seated Arab wearing a turban. Now she made another version with exaggerated facial features and a large head that gave it much more personality. This figure was issued as a bookend. She also modeled a cruet that consisted of a plate with a stylized duckling in the middle surrounded by egg cups. A frog resting under a mushroom was also issued as a bookend. All these pieces were issued with only Wilkinson's markings; Clarice's name was not included.

Colley was so pleased with the progress of her experiment that in the spring of 1928, after Clarice and Gladys had been working together for only several months and before a single piece of experimental ware had been sold, he added five apprentice girls to Clarice's staff. Clarice set up an efficient production system with her expanded team, giving the girls jobs of either outlining, enameling, or banding, according to their abilities. The following month Colley assigned two additional girls to Clarice, bringing her total staff to eight: Annie Berrisford, Mary Brown, Nellie Harrison, Clara Thomas, Nancy Liversage, Vera Rawlingson, Cissie Rhodes, and Gladys Scarlett.

By April the growing group was producing several different designs. Until this time each apprentice had herself chosen the pattern colors, but these were now standardized, and some were included in the Newport Pottery sample pattern book. Numbers S243 to S246 were shoulder designs of simple triangles on octagonal plates. Each consisted of a very limited number of colors within a black outline. Clarice instructed her girls to apply the paint thickly with exaggerated brushstrokes. This was the opposite of what apprentice decorators were normally taught, but Clarice felt that the roughness of the brushstrokes would make it more obvious that the ware was hand-painted.

A design from the PERSIAN (1) series on a 264 vase. 1928 or 1929.

The INSPIRATION (1) design on a HOLBORN shape bowl.
This was one of the first designs produced after the introduction of the ORIGINAL BIZARRE and dates from 1928.
The completely handwritten mark is pictured in the reference section on markings. Collection of Mrs. Betty Scott.

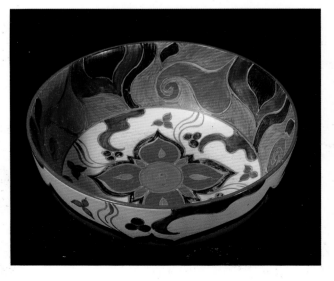

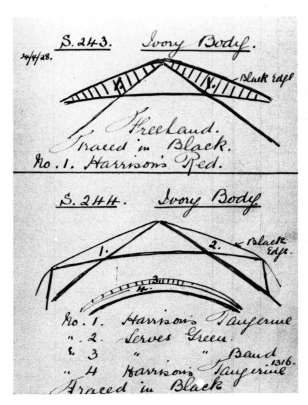

From the Newport Pottery samples book, the earliest designs in the ORIGINAL BIZARRE style.

Two of the earliest variations of the ORIGINAL BIZARRE designs. These drawings are from the pattern books used to copy designs for reorders.

A massive display of BIZARRE and LATONA ware in the window of Havens, a store in Leigh-on-Sea, in December 1929.

No attempt had yet been made to market any of Clarice's work. The growing stock of ware was simply stored at Newport Pottery. Clarice nevertheless must have been earning a handsome salary for that spring she learned to drive and paid sixty pounds for a brand new Austin Seven automobile. In contrast, the apprentice girls she supervised were earning less than two pounds a month. Around this time, Colley gave her more work space. Clarice retained her private studio at the Newport Pottery, next to Colley's office, but her girls were given their own shop in a storeroom in an adjacent warehouse. Clarice continued to work in her studio and look after the shop as well.

Some of the designs Clarice and her girls were producing were being issued with just Newport Pottery marks. Sample design 269, bold flowers and green leaves, painted onto toilet sets, became Newport pattern number 5667. At the same time, Clarice was helping Colley to produce a line of children's ware in order for Wilkinson's to compete with Shelley Potteries, which was highly successful with its children's line designed by Mabel Lucie Attwell.

In an event that was highly publicized at the time, Colley's eight-year-old daughter Joan unwittingly helped to design Wilkinson's new children's line. Colley took some of her drawings of matchstick men into the factory, showed them proudly to his workers, and then gave them to Clarice to adapt for the ware. The girls who actually produced the ware, Clarice's apprentices, were themselves only six or seven years older than Joan Shorter. Clarice herself designed a children's teapot called "Bones the Butcher," a "Blue Boy" milk jug, and a "Humpty Dumpty" sugar bowl.

In June Colley decided to test-market some of Clarice's work, choosing a few of the simpler geometric designs Clarice's girls had produced. Pattern S246, which Clarice had put in the Newport book in April, was issued as Wilkinson pattern number 8492. It was a shoulder decoration on an octagonal sandwich set, produced in tangerine and green.

The test-marketing results were positive, but the ware had been tested on such a small scale that there was not yet cause for celebration. Colley saw the need for careful planning and conferred with Clarice on strategies to improve their chances of success in a larger marketing effort. It was at this meeting that Clarice came up with the idea of giving her work an unusual name to attract attention. She chose the name *Bizarre* for her brash geometric designs, and in July 1928 her girls started writing this on the bottom of every piece.

Colley carefully planned a strategy to publicize *Bizarre*. His first advertisements reached the press in August, before the ware was on sale. They featured a tall candlestick and a plate decorated in a sharp geometric pattern. Colley's next idea was to stage a demonstration of the new ware. Such activities were often conducted by manufacturers to stimulate sales or bring new lines to the public's attention. Colley, Clarice, Gladys Scarlett, Nellie Harrison, and Florrie Winkle, a new addition to the *Bizarre* staff, traveled to London to put on a demonstration at the entrance to a major store. The girls demonstrated banding, lining, and enameling, and pieces of the finished ware were displayed on shelves behind the table where the girls were working. The press was invited, and photographs were taken of Clarice decorating some ware.

The next step, a crucial one, was to send out a large batch of ware with a salesman to see if it would sell. In September the salesman, Ewart Oakes, took *Bizarre* ware valued at two hundred pounds to the town of Reading in Berkshire; before the end of the week he was completely sold out. Colley's faith in Clarice had been vindicated.

Colley and Clarice, obviously delighted, immediately started arrangements for further production. More girls were hired, and Clarice worked even harder. She produced several variations on the triangles theme, as well as totally new designs. One featured a stylized

The first advertisement for BIZARRE ware, August 1928.

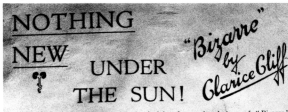

A 1929 advertisement for ARCHAIC ware.

Nellie Harrison, Florrie Winkle, Gladys Scarlett (painting the vase), and Clarice Cliff (painting a plate) give a demonstration of hand-painting at Waring and Gillows in London in August 1928.

The second advertisement for BIZARRE ware shows how rapidly the designs had advanced in the two months since the first advertisement had appeared.

One of Clarice's first attempts at photography, dating from late 1929, is this publicity shot of her BIZARRE ware.

tree, and another had an elaborate eastern style design. Late in 1928 Clarice issued a hand-painted version of the *Crocus* pattern, one that Wilkinson's had produced in lithograph form in 1925. Three or four simple, downward brushstrokes formed the petals of each flower, and thinner strokes formed the green leaves. This design was first decorated by Ethel Barrow, who was later aided by many other *Bizarre* girls when it became a best-seller.

All the basic geometric patterns had the *Bizarre* name handwritten on the bottom until, to speed up production, a *Bizarre* stamp was created. It was unusual for pottery companies to allow individual designers to put their names on the wares they produced, but in this case an exception was made. The stamp read, "Hand Painted *Bizarre* by Clarice Cliff, Newport Pottery, England."

Sales of Clarice's work continued to grow. More girls, and some boys, were hired until by the end of 1928 her staff numbered more than twenty-five. Clarice organized an efficient system, assigning decorators to benches according to their job. The front row of the shop was occupied by outliners, who, working with just one color, painted the basic pattern on the ware. Behind them sat the enamelers, whose job was to fill in the outline. Some shades, such as red and purple, had a consistency that made them difficult to apply evenly, so only certain girls worked with these. At the back of the shop were the banders and liners, who executed the last stage of decoration. They rotated the ware on a wheel with one hand, while with the other hand they brushed on a band of paint. Between each of these three stages the decorators would place the ware on wooden pallets at the side of the shop. From these the kilnman would carry boards full of completed pieces to the kilns for firing.

The demand on Clarice's time now was so great that she appointed a "missus" to supervise the running of the shop. Her name was Lily Slater, and her job was an important one. She made sure that all materials were on hand, that correct colors were available for each of the designs, and that apprentices properly mixed the powdered paint pigment with turpentine and oil. She also taught the apprentices how to apply the various brushstrokes, and, when samples were done, she made sure one of the girls spent an afternoon copying the designs into a pattern book. This was especially important because it insured that when orders arrived, ware could be produced in the same style. Even more important to Lily, however, was her responsibility in looking after the girls, helping them if they had personal problems or difficulty painting a complicated design. Both the girls and boys respected her greatly: she worked as hard as they did and was very popular. By the end of 1928 Clarice rarely visited the *Bizarre* shop more than twice a day, and Lily was therefore busy all the time.

An advertisement for Joan Shorter Baby Wear from 1928.

PERSIAN ISNIC style designs on INSPIRATION ware:
CONICAL rose bowl shape 400, twelve-inch LOTUS jug,
HAVRE shape bowl, vase shape 376, jardiniere shape 356.

The LATONA glazed ware in three different floral patterns:
a 264 vase, a plate, and a three-sided vase shape 200.
1929 or 1930.

The GREEN JAPAN design on a GREEK shape jug.
1933 or 1934.

## Chapter Four

n 1929 Clarice and Colley were to experience more success with the new *Bizarre* ware and with *Crocus* than they could ever have anticipated. New decorators were continually being hired and the production space greatly expanded. The *Bizarre* shop was extended into the storeroom area between the original shop and Clarice's private studio. In addition, warehouse space under the *Bizarre* shop and above the packing house at Newport was converted for the use of Clarice's staff. These latter areas were used exclusively for production of the enormously successful *Crocus*.

The ware was now being produced to a higher standard. In part, this occurred naturally as the girls gained more experience. Another reason for improved artistry, however, was that Clarice dropped her previous idea of having the girls exaggerate their brushstrokes. They were now instructed to keep the colors they applied as even as possible.

As sales increased, the original *Bizarre* designs continued to be produced on a variety of shapes, including *Lotus* jugs, *Athens* and globe-shape teapots, candlesticks, bowls, and vases. But in early 1929 Clarice was also busy modeling new vase and bowl shapes. As the stock of Newport ware she had used to launch *Bizarre* was depleted, shapes that were very old-fashioned were replaced with new ones designed by Clarice.

As a source of inspiration for new designs, Clarice had for some time been subscribing to *Mobilier et Décoration*, a monthly French design journal. She was especially impressed with the work of Robert Lallemant. Clarice felt that his round and square vases, often tiered, would be perfect for her *Bizarre* designs. She soon started modeling shapes based on them, such as numbers 366 to 369. Shape 370 was a globe-shaped vase, identical to one pictured in *Mobilier et Décoration*. During 1929 Clarice also produced some other vases with clean futuristic lines, including shape numbers 358 to 365.

Clarice was very much aware of the need to appeal to a full range of tastes, so, in addition to her avant-garde work she also designed traditional shapes. The idea for her series of traditional vases, called the *Archaic* series, came to Clarice from a book by Owen Jones entitled *The Grammar of Ornament*, which pictured classic architectural columns with modeled tops. Clarice decorated her vases with designs virtually identical to those from Jones's book. Since the outlining on the *Archaic* pieces is quite complicated, the ware was expensive when marketed, which may have been why it sold only in small quantities. The shapes Clarice had specially modeled for the series, however, numbers 372 and 374 to 377, became part of the standard *Bizarre* range for several years and were issued with many of the later designs on them.

A BEEHIVE honeypot in CROCUS and a chrome topped
honeypot in CHINTZ ORANGE.

In April and May Clarice produced some unusual shapes based on cones with either triangular feet or triangular handles. Her inspiration was a conical bowl with three triangular feet that had been produced in silver by the French designer Desny. The range produced by Clarice was originally called *Odilon*, but she later changed the name to *Conical*.

She produced *Conical* bowls in various sizes and configurations. Her basic *Conical* bowl shape supported by four triangular legs, number 383, is a masterpiece of design. Other notable pieces in this series include the *Yo Yo* vase, shape number 379, which is similar to a silver goblet produced by Desny, although Clarice marketed it as a flower holder. Also in the *Conical* series are candlestick 384, a small conical bowl with a fitment to hold a candle; shape 400, which serves as the basis for both a rose bowl and a biscuit jar; and shape 380, which has one conical bowl inside another so that flowers can be arranged on two levels. Some shapes in the *Conical* series were startlingly different from anything else being produced in the Potteries at the time. These included a teapot with triangles for handle and spout, cream and sugar containers with triangular feet, and a cup with a solid triangle for a handle. Newspaper critics praised the introduction of this avant-garde tea set, and it became extraordinarily popular.

Some pieces in the *Conical* series were issued with a new glaze Clarice called *Latona*, a smooth, matte, milky glaze as opposed to the shiny, honeyglaze traditionally used by Wilkinson's. Clarice also produced special *Latona* designs. An example is *Latona Red Roses*, a pattern the *Bizarre* girls made by tracing the design in India ink and then filling in red roses and black leaves, imparting the effect of colors being stencilled on. *Latona Tree* was another of the early landscapes. It featured a rainbow-colored tree with smaller trees on either side.

In the latter part of 1929, Clarice created a number of interesting designs that soon became enormously popular. These included sample 514, an abstract design in black, tangerine, and chrome green that became Newport pattern number 5799 and was named *Ravel*. *Ravel*, a shoulder pattern introduced in late 1929, remained in production throughout most of the 1930s. Also produced in late 1929 was another of Clarice's earliest landscapes, sample 524. It shows a single-windowed cottage nestled between a bush, formed of bubbles, and two fir trees. Clarice later based her *Trees and House* design on this design.

In addition to developing new shapes and designs, Clarice also experimented with new production techniques. Colley had for some time been interested in producing quality art pottery using high-fired oxide glazes in what were known as Egyptian Scarab blue glazes. His technicians had carried out experiments, and the results were excellent. He aimed the ware, introduced under the name of *Inspiration*, at a discriminating, up-scale market.

The *Inspiration* production process was complicated. While still in the green clay state, the ware was covered in a clear glaze and fired at low temperature, which gave it a rough surface on which Ellen Browne outlined the design. It was extremely difficult to decorate on this surface, so patterns were outlined very broadly. Some of Clarice's girls remember having to wrap their fingertips in tape to protect them from the rough surface of the ware.

The materials used for *Inspiration* were also difficult to work with. Raw oxides of copper, cobalt, and iron were used to produce the distinctive blues, lilacs, and mauves. These oxide solutions had the consistency of water, however, and thus decorating with them was a

Clarice Cliff inspecting an INSPIRATION LOTUS jug in the Newport Pottery showroom in 1929.

Ellen Browne and Gladys Scarlett on the steps of the Russell Square Ladies Club, where they stayed while they did a demonstration in London in 1929.

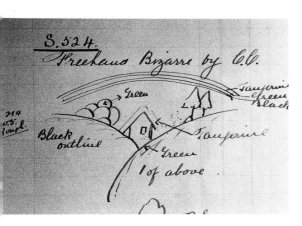

From the Newport Pottery samples book of May 1929, a rough sketch for the TREES AND HOUSE design, issued in 1930.

An advertisement for BIZARRE ware that ran in Australia in 1929.

very messy business. Also, the glazes were very volatile and could be ruined by contact with other materials.

After the oxides were applied, the piece was fired at a temperature much higher than that used for firing the on-glaze colors of *Bizarre* ware. Firing often caused the oxide glazes to run over the kiln furniture, joining it to the pottery. This made it necessary to carefully disengage the pottery from the kiln furniture and grind down the resultant marks, a time-consuming process. Also, the kiln furniture was usually ruined and had to be replaced for the next firing.

*Inspiration* was launched in September 1929. The high costs, the two firings, and a high failure rate meant that it was twice as expensive as normal *Bizarre* ware: it was priced at about twenty-three shillings, nearly four weeks' wages for a *Bizarre* girl. The price, however, made it the company's most prestigious line.

Some of the early *Inspiration* pieces included simple floral and Isnic patterns and a landscape. One of the first new shapes the *Inspiration* glaze was used on was a large, Cubist-style face mask designed by a boy apprentice, Ron Birks.

In late 1929 Clarice also created some adventurous new *Bizarre* patterns that moved completely away from the basic geometrics originally used for the *Bizarre* series. One of these was *Sunray*, a three-part design of black, stylized skyscrapers with a bridge, clouds, and a sunburst between them. Another startling design in this series, created in the Art Deco style, is one we will call *Lightning*; the original name is lost. It has a thick, black zig-zag between blue circles and striped triangles. Although innovative designs such as these were not good sellers—most customers would admire them and then buy something with a more conservative pattern—they did excite interest in *Bizarre* ware, which is what Colley Shorter wanted. Again and again during the *Bizarre* years, his protégée would produce shapes and designs that served to provide publicity for the more conservative patterns that formed the bread-and-butter output of the Pottery—patterns such as *Crocus* and *Ravel*.

By October 1929 Newport Pottery, thanks to Clarice, was making such large profits that Colley had to divert some sales to Wilkinson's in order to avoid heavy tax bills. He did this by issuing a new series of *Bizarre*-style designs under a different trade name classed as the output of Wilkinson's. Clarice resorted to her by-now extensive library of books to choose the new trade name; since "fantastic" was one of the dictionary definitions of bizarre, she called the new lines *Fantasque*. The back-stamp was identical to the one used for *Bizarre* except that the word "Fantasque" written in script was substituted for *Bizarre*.

Clarice put together eight designs for the first *Fantasque* series. These were some of the first to have actual design names; previously patterns were sold under the umbrella title *Bizarre*. The first *Fantasque* range consisted of *Fruit*, *Lily*, *Cherries*, *Kandina*, *Caprice*, *Broth*, and two other designs, the names of which are not known. All sold well, but the most successful was *Broth*, which continued in production long after the others. The *Fantasque* series was in the shops by late 1929 and was produced in a variety of old and new shapes. Clarice's ware was now in such high demand that virtually anything with her name on it sold well.

The year 1929 was a period of enormous activity for Clarice. By now the entire Newport Pottery had been converted to the exclusive use of Clarice and her continuously growing staff. Still Clarice, who was not really an artist but an industrial designer, felt driven to create more diverse designs to cater to the full range of tastes of the buying public. For Clarice, 1930 would prove even more active.

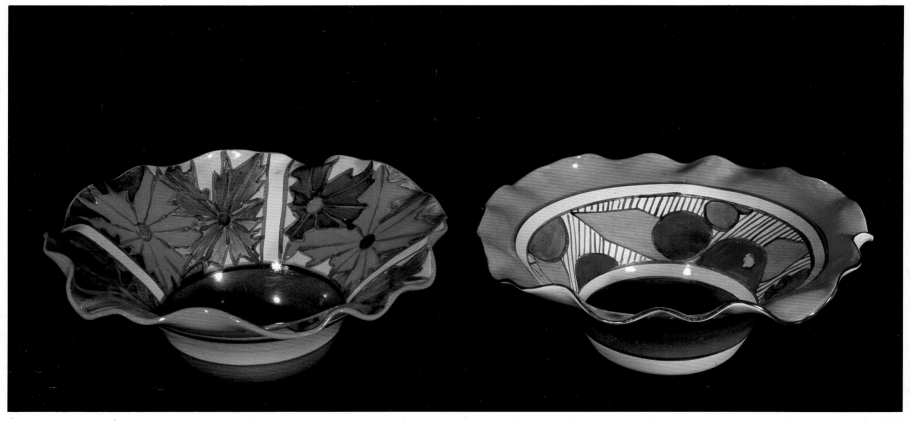

Two POPPY bowls in early FANTASQUE designs (1929 or 1930). The POPPY bowl was an old Newport shape.

The CUBIST design on a 373 vase originally made for the ARCHAIC series, and a twelve-inch LOTUS jug. 1929 or 1930.

# Chapter Five
## 1930

The BUTTERFLY design on an ISIS jug. This was copied from a design by Edouard Benedictus. 1930.

o china or pottery manufacturer in the Stoke-on-Trent area could match the success and sales that Newport and Wilkinson's were experiencing at the start of 1930. *Bizarre, Fantasque, Inspiration*, and *Latona* were all selling well, and the factory could not keep up with the demand for *Crocus*. The kilns were manned twenty-four hours a day.

Clarice became even more prolific, producing in 1930 new shapes and designs and expanding the *Bizarre, Fantasque, Inspiration*, and *Latona* ranges, which were all still regarded as separate lines. New *Fantasque* patterns appeared in the early months of the year. A design called *Melon* featured fruit drawn in Cubist style and outlined in brown. *Fantasque Trees and House*, introduced at the same time, represents Clarice's first proper landscape. Based on design number S524, which Clarice had done in May of 1929, it shows a landscape drawn in silhouette with trees in wedge and bubble shapes and a half-hidden cottage.

Other *Fantasque* patterns introduced in the first part of 1930 have adventurous abstract designs with wavy lines, circles, and squares boldly covering the ware. They make the original *Bizarre* look conservative by comparison. Clarice's new designs exhibited a lot more style and flow than the earlier ones, and the French influence on her work became more evident.

The success of the *Conical* teapot by early 1930 spurred Clarice to add a coffeepot to her line. Small coffee cups with triangular handles and the creamer and sugar container from the *Conical* teaware completed the set. In April and May larger sizes of the *Conical* teapot were introduced. Although the original size continued with a solid triangular handle, the four- and six-cup sized teapots were produced with an open handle to accommodate the heavier weight. The numbers on the base of these teapots are not shape numbers, but refer to the number of pieces of ware that could be packed into a standard kiln container. Thus, the smallest sized conical teapot is a "42," the medium a "36," and the large a "24."

While the mold-making shop underneath Clarice's studio was producing the new shapes for the *Conical* ware, Clarice was busy supervising experiments on a new style of decoration, covering ware with "runnings" in various colors. The ware was roughly banded with enamel colors thinned with turpentine, starting at the bottom with one color, and then working up with different ones; the thinned enamel ran down the sides of the ware. When the desired effect was achieved, the decorators fanned the ware with large sheets of cardboard to dry the enamel and stop the running.

An original Edouard Benedictus design produced by the POCHOIR process and issued as part of his Nouvelles Variations folio in 1926. Clarice purchased a copy of this in 1927 and copied elements of at least eight of the designs in work she produced in late 1929 and 1930. The castle turrets and triangular trees in this example appear in APPLIQUE LUCERNE.

The BIZARRE shop pictured in the DAILY SKETCH on December 4, 1931.

The Jean Tetard shapes on which the STAMFORD teaset
was based.

An advertisement for ORIGINAL DELICIA, displayed on the
special stand Clarice designed and patented in 1930.

Clarice called this style of decoration *Delecia*. Early pieces were produced with the mark "Hand painted *Delecia* by Clarice Cliff," with *Delecia* in script. The running effect was to be used again in the following years, when it was combined with hand-painted fruit or flowers, but the original *Delecia* was rarely produced after 1930.

During April and May, Clarice created new designs, some of which were the most highly decorated ware she produced. She called the series *Applique*, a French name possibly chosen because her designs were inspired by the work of a French designer, Edouard Benedictus. Clarice had seen illustrations of his work in folios that were published with the intention that the designer be paid a commission by anyone using the designs. Clarice does not appear to have done this.

The first two *Applique* designs inspired by Benedictus were landscapes with mountains and trees. *Lucerne* featured a castle and *Lugano* a waterwheel. The castle turrets and trees in *Lucerne* and the buildings in *Lugano* are identical to the Benedictus originals, and the overall composition of the landscape was also copied. Other floral and abstract designs from the Benedictus folios were also used by Clarice for the *Bizarre* range, but it was by emulating the all-over color of his landscapes that Clarice produced some of her best pieces in *Applique*.

It appears that these pieces were perhaps too garish for the average buyer in 1930, and although they were still being ordered as late as 1933, they were never sold in great quantities. The highly decorated *Applique* pieces were expensive to produce, costing more than the standard *Fantasque* and *Bizarre* ranges. For example, a small *Conical* teapot cost three shillings in a *Fantasque* pattern and four in an *Applique* pattern.

Although *Applique* and *Delecia* were more startling, the best-selling line during 1930 and for most of the decade was *Crocus*. Colley soon encouraged Clarice to

A lamp base, decorated in the FOOTBALL design, which
Clarice was inspired to produce after seeing the work of
Robert Lallement.

An Edouard Benedictus landscape that obviously
influenced some of Clarice Cliff's APPLIQUE designs.

An unused ink drawing by Clarice Cliff, probably intended to be used on the cover of a brochure.

A press picture of Clarice "painting" some AGE OF JAZZ figures.

An advertising photograph by Clarice Cliff showing the AGE OF JAZZ figures.

diversify the line. She produced a pattern called *Gayday*, which has the same banding as *Crocus* but has large asters in between the bands. *Gayday* quickly became popular and was produced alongside *Crocus* for several years.

Less popular but especially interesting were a series of figures that Clarice produced in the summer of 1930. Her *Age of Jazz* series is the most reminiscent of Art Deco of all Clarice's work. She found in *Age of Jazz* a way to produce figures—always her special interest—that would be a suitable addition to her *Bizarre* range. Clarice silhouetted figures out of a sheet of clay and fixed these to a base, taking the idea from a 1929 edition of *Mobilier et Décoration* that illustrated some Robert Lallemant tree silhouettes.

Clarice used the silhouette theme to produce dancing couples and musicians. There were five in the series: numbers 432 and 433 each depict a single dancing couple; 434 shows two couples dancing; 435 depicts a drummer and trumpeter; and 436 a pianist and banjo player. The women are in colorful gowns, the men in black-and-white evening wear. These *Age of Jazz* figures were unlike anything produced before: they were almost adult toys.

Clarice also produced that same summer cut-out flowers using the same technique, designed to stand in sand in her tiered vases. Her *Pansies* are number 438 and *Tulips* are 439. Eventually Clarice would copy Lallemant directly by producing some cut-out trees.

She did not rest with the success of her silhouettes, however. Clarice, in a flurry of activity, created new designs for a major exhibition to be held in September. At Colley's urging, she designed a new teapot shape, once again turning to the pages of *Mobilier et Décoration* for ideas. There she found an illustration of an award-winning silver teapot designed by Jean Tetard. She felt it might have as much sales potential as her *Conical* shape and promptly copied it in clay. It was a complicated process as the shape had so many edges, but the only change she made from Tetard's original form was to put an open handle on the teapot. Eventually Tetard discovered that Clarice had copied his idea, and Colley had to buy the rights to his design.

Clarice decided to call the new shape *Stamford*. Now, with the addition of cups and saucers from the *Conical* ware, she had a new early-morning set. She decorated the *Stamford* ware in some of her newest patterns, including *Trees and House* and *Melon*, and it was launched along with *Age of Jazz* in the September exhibition in London.

At the exhibition, she used *Age of Jazz* figures as part of a tableware display in which plates, candlesticks, and conical bowls were all painted black with red detail. The effect was startling, and the press gave extensive coverage to Clarice's wares. It was the *Stamford* teapot, however, that was the success of the exhibition. Few of the *Age of Jazz* figures sold, but orders poured in for the teapot.

After the exhibition Clarice created a special stand for *Bizarre* ware. A huge, tiered, semicircular stand with "Bizarre by Clarice Cliff" stamped on it was produced and patented. Although the stand was used in publicity pictures, it does not appear to have been produced for retailers in any large quantity.

In October Clarice added new designs to her *Applique* range. *Avignon* features a river, bridge, and bushes; *Palermo* has yachts with red sails in a bay surrounded by mountains; another design has a windmill in a river landscape; *Bird of Paradise* shows an exotic bird perched among leaves and berries. Some of these pieces move away from the "all-over" painting style of the original *Applique*, a style that was more time-consuming and therefore more expensive.

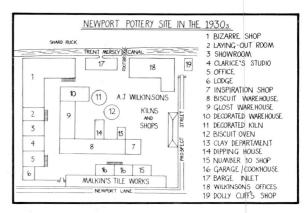

A graphic display of the floor plan of the Newport Pottery. In reality Wilkinson's buildings occupied a far greater area; the Newport facility has been enlarged here for clarity.

One of Clarice's own publicity shots of a LUGANO charger and a LOTUS jug, also showing two versions of the Arab bookends.

Clarice Cliff and a Lord Mayor inspecting a piece of INSPIRATION at a trade show in 1930.

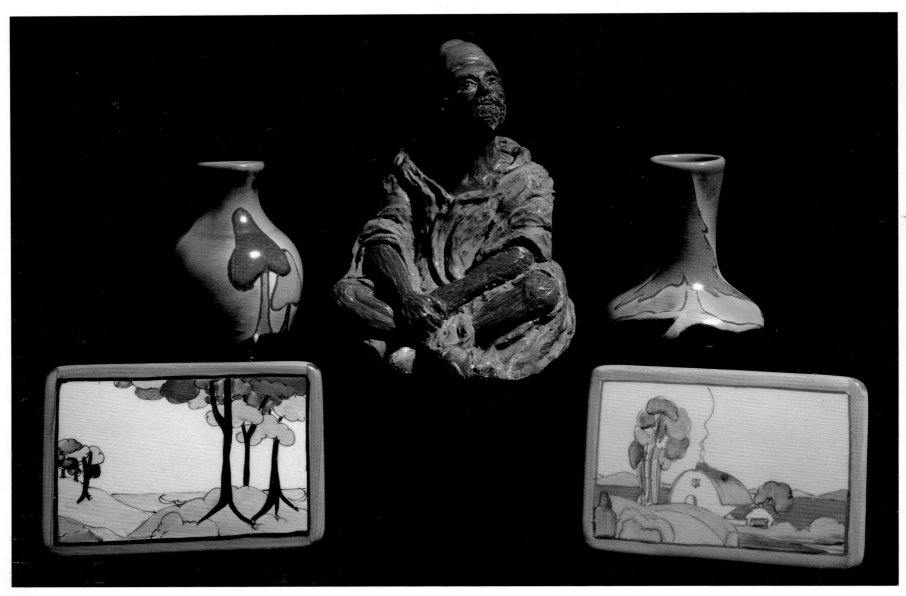

Clarice Cliff rarities. The Arab figure, the earliest piece of Clarice Cliff ware known, was handmade by her in 1924. Clarice gave it to Hilda Lovatt in the 1960s. It was probably the original from which Clarice had the idea for the molded Arab figures used for bookends. The handmade mark and date on its base are pictured in the reference section on markings. On either side of the figure is a pair of MINIATURE VASES in INSPIRATION CAPRICE, each only two inches high. A set of four miniature vases sold as shape 177 are particularly interesting as they are of extremely good quality and have the whole of the mark handwritten on the base. It is believed that Clarice had them specially produced for a friend. Also pictured are two rare ADVERTISING PLAQUES. These are just two and a half inches high and were not introduced until 1934. They were designed to use in shops to illustrate other colorways and designs the ware was available in. Both have handwritten marks on the reverse: "BRIDGEWATER BY CLARICE CLIFF" and "BLUE FIRS BY CLARICE CLIFF."
Collections of David and Pauline Latham and Leonard Griffin.

A selection of vases in INSPIRATION designs. From the left: a 369 vase, a 379 YO YO vase, a 378 vase, and a 279 vase.

Other patterns that appeared around this time were *Fantasque Berries*, which showed red and orange berries next to a green and yellow geometric motif, and *Green House*, a very powerful pattern on the trees and cottage theme. To the *Bizarre* range Clarice added some designs once again inspired by her collection of French designers' work. From *Mobilier et Décoration*, a Robert Lallemant shape was adapted to a flat-sided, oblong lamp base. She also copied line for line a carpet design by Ivan DaSilva Bruhns. More Edouard Benedictus designs were also used. One has a stylized butterfly against a striped background, and another incorporates a motif resembling shark's teeth. A Benedictus floral pattern of stylized bell-shaped flowers with curled tendrils above them was also copied. None of these patterns were good sellers. Though Clarice was adventurous in transferring these patterns to pottery, the conservative British buyer stuck mainly to *Crocus* and *Gayday*.

It was toward the end of 1930 that Clarice introduced another new shape, this one called *Eton*. The tall coffeepot and teapot were each composed of a tube-shaped body, square lid, and diamond-shaped handle. Eventually a jug was added, but it was not a major success. *Conical* accessories were therefore used to complete the set. The *Eton* shape was in production for several years until it was phased out, probably in 1934.

In the latter months of 1930, the factory made a change in the by now impressive accumulation of back stamps used to mark Clarice's pottery. *Bizarre*, *Delecia*, *Fantasque*, and *Lodore* all had marks with the name in script. *Applique*, *Latona*, and *Crocus* often had the design name handwritten above a *Bizarre* mark. Starting in August 1930, all the ware was issued with a mark that included the word *Bizarre*. The *Fantasque* mark with the name in script was replaced with *Fantasque* printed in block letters, followed by "Hand Painted *Bizarre* by Clarice Cliff." This mark was in use for approximately one year. By this time production of the simple geometric designs originally issued under the *Bizarre* name had virtually ceased in favor of more elaborate ones. Now *Bizarre* was used as an umbrella title for all Clarice's wares.

The factory was busier than ever in the months leading up to Christmas of 1930, trying to fill their huge volume of orders. Clarice found more and more demands being made on her and delegated much of her work. She still found time, however, to take the publicity pictures of her ware personally in her small photography studio at Newport. She retained her love of photography but by 1931 she would have to give it up as the demands on her time grew even heavier.

Colley Shorter relaxing at Llangollen.

Among those boarding a Llangollen bus are: front row, Doris Bailey, Wilkinson painter Maria Green, Edith Walton, Nellie Harrison (eating apple), Ellen Browne, Ivy Stringer, Laura Bossons; second row, Betty Henshall, Annie Jackson, Lily Slater (hidden at the back), Elsie Devon (behind Nellie Harrison), Nancy Liversage, and Sadie Maskery.

Winnie Davis and Elsie Devon relaxing on a wall at Newport Pottery during a break from work at the BIZARRE shop.

Abstract floral designs on INSPIRATION ware: a rose bowl shape 234, a plate, a HOLBORN shape bowl, a LOTUS jug with orange overpainting, and a ginger jar shape 132.

Opposite:
Abstract floral designs on INSPIRATION ware: a rose bowl shape 234
and a shape 14 vase decorated in NASTURTIUM,
one of the later pieces of INSPIRATION, dating from 1932.

Candlesticks: a pair of 391 shape decorated in the CLOUVRE design (1930),
a small OCTAGONAL in the INSPIRATION CAPRICE design, a large OCTAGONAL in an INSPIRATION floral design,
and an old Newport candlestick in an ORIGINAL BIZARRE pattern. All produced before 1931.

Examples of the FANTASQUE GARDENIA design: shape 14 vase, 264 vase, eighteen-inch charger, square bowl 367, LOTUS jug.

Opposite:
The APPLIQUE PALERMO design, on twelve-inch vase shape 374,
which was originally produced as part of the ARCHAIC shape range.
This example dates from 1930.

Two of the five figures from the AGE OF JAZZ series: shape 436, a pianist and a banjo player, and shape 432, a dancing couple. 1930. Collection of Mrs. Betty Scott.

The FLOWER AND SQUARES design on a twin-handled LOTUS jug. 1930 or 1931.

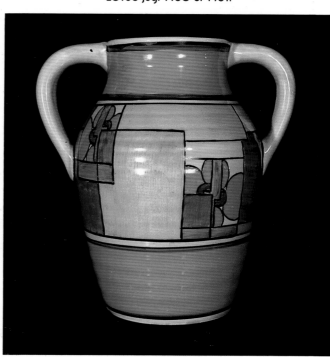

## Chapter Six
## 1931

An INSPIRATION floral design
on a 342 shape vase.

T he Newport and Wilkinson's staffs were in a fortunate position in 1931. The Western world was in the depths of the Great Depression, and unemployment in the Potteries exceeded 20 percent. Thanks to the spectacular success of *Bizarre* ware, however, Clarice's staff not only had secure employment, their salaries were actually being increased.

Clarice was busier than ever expanding the line. In early 1931 she issued two new *Fantasque* landscape patterns that featured trees and houses. Both patterns were good sellers. One design, *Autumn*, features a cottage partly hidden by bushes, with huge, bulbous, sinuous-trunked trees towering above. Until the *Autumn* name was discovered recently, collectors referred to this design as "Balloon Trees." *Autumn* was first produced in the *Trees and House* shades of red, green, and black, but Clarice soon adapted it to make the trees blue, green, and yellow. The following year it was replaced with the *Pastel Autumn* and *Orange Autumn* versions. Clarice's second new *Fantasque* pattern was called *Summerhouse*. This features an exotic landscape with green-stemmed trees adorned with bulbous yellow foliage. Adjacent to the trees are a red hut and a blue pool. *Summerhouse* was originally issued with red banding, but soon came out with other variations, orange banding the most common. Otherwise *Summerhouse*, unlike *Autumn*, was never produced in a variety of color patterns.

In addition to expanding the *Fantasque* line, Clarice introduced two new designs that combined the *Inspiration* glaze with hand-painting: *Marigold* and *Clouvre*. After the piece was outlined, the *Inspiration* glaze was applied to all parts of the ware except that part that was to take the pattern. The piece was then fired. The plain area was then painted on glaze and the piece was refired. Because of the two firings the ware was expensive, which may explain why neither design was produced for very long.

The quality of the wares produced in the *Bizarre* shop was ultimately the responsibility of the outliners. Adapting designs to round or square, high or low shapes was not always easy. The outliners worked closely with Clarice to adapt her designs to the various shapes, for she designed on paper. There is also some evidence that Clarice was influenced by the designs her outliners had produced at their evening classes. The exercise books of outliners Ellen Browne and Harold Walker, which mainly predate the *Bizarre* years, have

A spill vase, shape number 194
in a PERSIAN (2) design.
1930 or 1931.

**Opposite:**
The INSPIRATION ASTER design on an ISIS vase, a
twenty-four-inch-high umbrella stand (the largest known
Cliff piece), a globe vase 370, and a 360 vase. The
design was introduced in 1930.

An abstract INSPIRATION design on a 367 shape bowl.

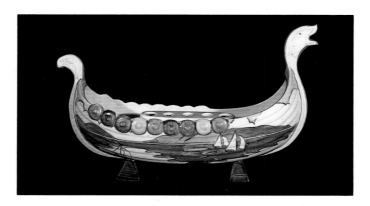

Three pieces from the ARCHAIC series, based on designs from THE GRAMMAR OF ORNAMENT by Owen Jones, introduced in 1929. From the left: shape 375, shape 374, shape 373. Height of largest piece: twelve inches.

Opposite, above:
Two colorways of the same design. HONOLULU has the
orange-and-yellow tree, RUDYARD the blue-and-pink one.
From the left: vase 452, vase 358, DAFFODIL bowl shape
450, vase 451 with castellated rim, CONICAL bowl 384, ISIS vase.

Opposite, middle:
VIKING BOAT, sixteen inches long, decorated in the
GIBRALTAR pattern. The VIKING BOAT shape was
introduced in 1927; this piece dates from 1931 or 1932.

Opposite, below:
The AUTUMN design in its BLUE and PASTEL colorways and
another variant, a STAMFORD shape water jug, a 365 vase,
a 132 GINGER JAR, and two twelve-inch LOTUS jugs.

An early morning set in a version of the TENNIS design. 1931.

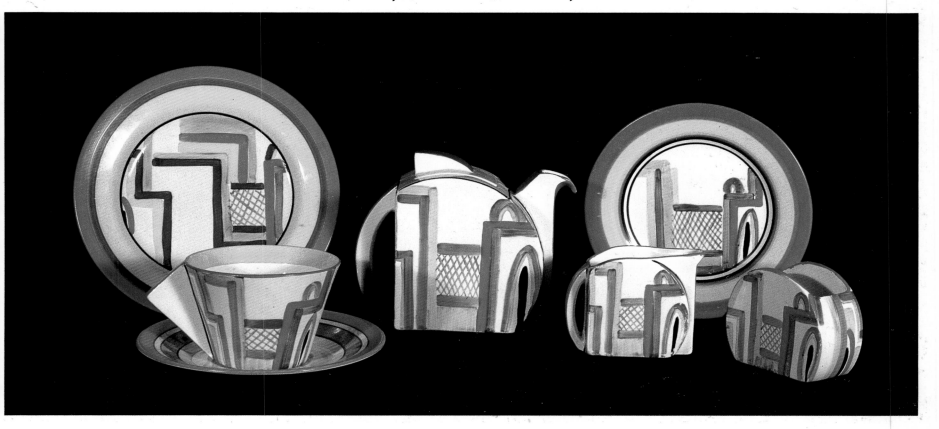

An undated design from one of Harold Walker's sketchbooks, showing many AGE OF JAZZ design elements.

A sketch from one of Ellen Browne's 1928 design books. The turretted buildings strongly resemble those in Clarice Cliff's ALTON design of 1933.

many designs very similar to the landscape or abstract patterns Clarice produced. Indeed, pattern 6140 from the factory's pattern book is listed as "Hand-painted scenes by Harold Walker." Clarice acknowledged in an interview in 1931 that much of her success was due to her workers: "I have several boy apprentices now, and one, who is just 16, seems to have inherited brilliant artistic qualities from his father and grandfather, who were artists in the Potteries years ago."

Unusual new shapes that Clarice issued in early 1931 added to her reputation for being innovative. Vase numbers 460 and 461 and bowl 515 are very similar to some of Robert Lallemant's work that was featured in 1929 editions of *Mobilier et Décoration*. Clarice, however, produced so many different styles in 1931 that many of the designs must have been entirely her own. Other shapes issued around this time include bowl number 450 and dish number 475, part of a new shape range called *Daffodil*. Several flower tube vases that combine flat clay feet with tubes to hold water (464, 465, and 511) and some *Stamford* bowls and tureens (441, 442, and 443) were also produced.

The most unusual item to emerge from Newport Pottery in 1931 was a five-foot-high horse made entirely of *Bizarre* ware. Clarice previously had made an ink sketch of this horse for publicity purposes, but Colley had not before seen fit to take it into production, possibly because producing it was not a simple matter. Prior to glazing, holes had to be drilled in *Bizarre* ware so that they could be fitted onto a specially made iron frame. Candlesticks formed the legs, *Globe* vases the knee joints, a large umbrella stand the body, and various vases formed the neck. A felt pad was inserted between each piece to prevent breakage. Two thirteen-inch plaques with a large black eye painted on each were mounted on either side of the head.

Clarice initially called the horse "Miss *Bizarre*," but Colley decided to name the horse the *Bizooka*. The first *Bizooka* was taken to exhibitions and loaned to shops for window displays. It was so successful that Colley had four more made. These toured not only Great Britain but New Zealand and Australia and received newspaper coverage as far off as the United States.

Although not as flamboyant as the *Bizooka*, another interesting piece was created by Clarice in August of 1931—the *Conical* sugar dredger. It seems unusual that having originally designed the *Conical* range in mid-1929, Clarice should have taken two years to add the dredger, but it proved to be a good seller.

Clarice Cliff in a press photograph taken in her studio in 1931. The picture has obviously been posed, as she could not have been holding an unfired charger against her overalls to paint without smudging it.

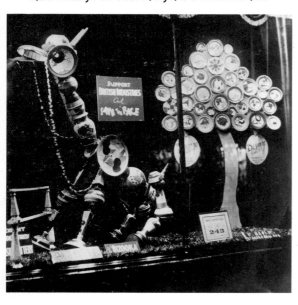

The BIZOOKA, pictured in 1931 in the window of Haven's store in Leigh-on-Sea. At right is a BIZARRE tree.

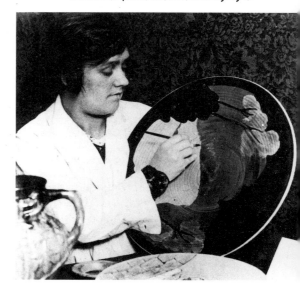

Drawing of Harold Walker's CAR & SKYSCRAPER design, never produced commercially.

The SOLITUDE design on an ISIS vase, BLUE FIRS on a DAFFODIL shape bowl (450) and a YO YO vase (379).

Also in the summer of 1931, further changes were made in the back-stamps applied to the ware: a series of printed lithograph marks replaced the stamped marks. The lithograph marks were clearer and finer than the stamp marks and obviously could not be smudged. The marks were produced on lithograph sheets that, in addition to the words "Hand Painted *Bizarre* by Clarice Cliff, Newport Pottery, England," have design or range names in block letters. Lithograph marks were made for *Crocus, Delecia, Fantasque*, and *Gayday*, as well as for two styles newly introduced in the summer of 1931, *Cafe-au-Lait* and *Nuage*. They were not made for *Inspiration* and *Latona* because production in these ranges was minimal by 1931. A lithograph mark also was made for *Applique*, but it was rarely used for original *Applique* designs; rather, it was confined to entirely different designs that did not appear until 1932.

To produce the *Cafe-au-Lait* style, already glazed ware was completely covered with stippled background color, created by applying the paint with a sponge. Then standard *Bizarre* or *Fantasque* designs were applied over the stippling. The name *Cafe-au-Lait* is sometimes misleading because although the stippled background effect is most commonly seen in a brown shade, it was also done in blue, green, yellow, and orange. One could, for example, order a *Cafe-au-Lait* vase decorated with the *Autumn* pattern and choose a background shade to match a particular room decor. The stippling effect widened the appeal of the ware yet, because it took only a few seconds to apply the paint with a sponge, was not an expensive process.

*Nuage* ware shows a similar stippled effect. It differs from *Cafe-au-Lait* in that the paint used was mixed with a thickener to give the surface of the ware the texture of the rind of an orange. *Nuage* also displays individual designs over the stippling—the designs are of stenciled flowers or fruit—and the ware is not banded.

Also in 1931 Clarice created her new *Daffodil* shape range of coffee and tea ware. These pieces have sinuous lines reminiscent of Art Nouveau. They were initially issued in simple floral designs that allowed the strength of the shapes to assert themselves and were also produced in an equally well-suited, delicate pink glaze called *Damask Rose*. Eventually, however, customers in the 1930s ordered the ware with full landscape patterns, which look incongruous combined with these strong, sinuous shapes.

A 363 vase in the TENNIS design, a 452 vase in TULIP, a double BON JOUR shape candlestick in SECRETS, an oval BON JOUR vase in ORANGE ROOF COTTAGE, an old Newport shape BEEHIVE covered bowl.

Some of Clarice's most typical landscape patterns were introduced toward the end of 1931. *Red Roofs* is a rural scene showing a house with an orange flowering plant climbing its walls. *Farmhouse*, one of Clarice's best cottage and trees themes, is a particularly strong pattern produced in shades of orange, amber, yellow, and green. Around the same time Clarice also introduced *House and Bridge*. It features Clarice's usual tree and cottage scene, only in more detail. The effect of the ware, finished in black, red, and orange banding, is quite startling, and the design sold well on a variety of shapes. It was phased out around early 1933.

Clarice also created a new seascape in late 1931. Her previous *Applique Palermo* pattern, which featured yachts on a sea, had not sold well. This time she used the same theme but viewed it from the sea, using the Rock of Gibraltar as a backdrop. She called the new pattern *Gibraltar* and produced it in a blend of sugary pink, lilac, blue, yellow, and mauve. Neither *House and Bridge* nor *Gibraltar* is known in any other color variation.

The *Bizarre* shop was very busy during the Christmas season of 1931, and despite the Great Depression Colley was prospering. His happiness over his business success and his relationship with Clarice might have been muted, however, by his home life. His marriage had become an unhappy one, and he was very distant from his two daughters. He turned instead to the world of *Bizarre*, *Bizookas*, and *Fantasque* that he had built with Clarice; he found much at his factory to keep his mind occupied, for the enormous success of *Bizarre* ware was to continue into 1932.

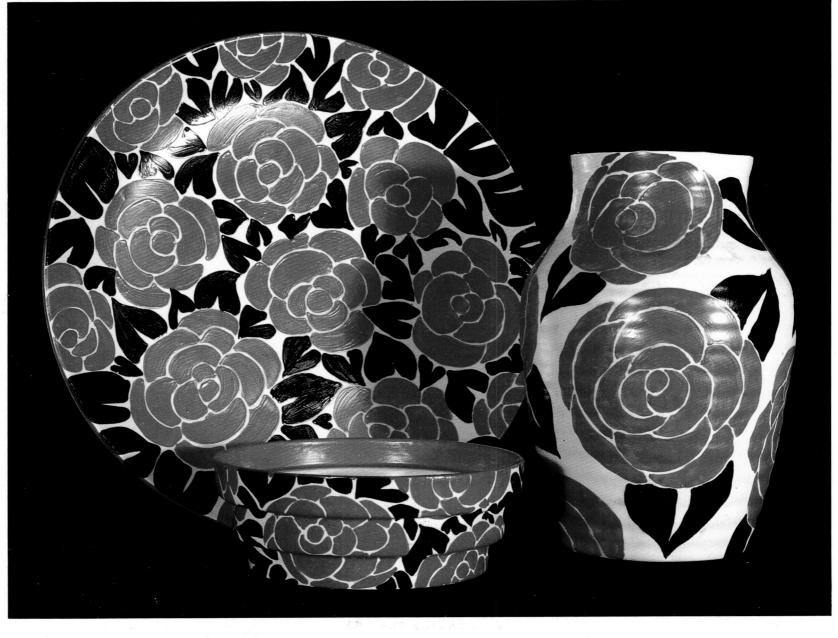

## Chapter Seven
## 1932

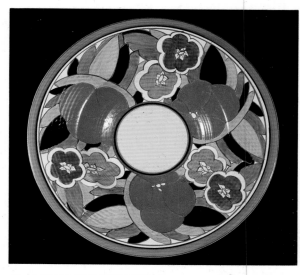

The FANTASQUE MOUNTAIN design on a thirteen-inch wall plaque. 1931.

**D**uring this busiest of the *Bizarre* years, Clarice produced many new shapes. Florally, *Nasturtium, Canterbury Bells, Sungay, Chintz, Hollyrose,* and *Marguerite* all appeared in 1932. This latter range features simple body shapes finished in *Cafe-au-Lait* stipple with modeled flowers as handles. *Marguerite* sold quite well, and Clarice would turn to the concept again, even more successfully, in 1934.

Clarice was equally prolific in creating new patterns in 1932. Fruit inspired the patterns of *Apples, Delecia Citrus, Oranges & Lemons,* and *Pastel Melon.* New landscapes included *Limberlost, Poplar, Pink Roof Cottage, Orange Roof Cottage, Moonlight, May Avenue, Pastel Autumn,* and *Orange Autumn.* A garden scene with a woman in a crinoline dress called *Idyll* was issued with an *Applique* mark. *Idyll* bore no relation to the style of the original *Applique* but was probably included as part of that range because it used many colors. It was also more expensive than standard *Fantasque* or *Bizarre.* Most of Clarice's new landscapes, however, were in true *Bizarre* style and, in her usual eclectic manner, she chose names for them from diverse sources. *May Avenue,* for example, was an actual tree-lined road just a few miles from the factory, and *Limberlost* was taken from *Girl of the Limberlost,* a popular book and film of the time.

In addition to new vase shapes and patterns, Clarice also added more amusing animals to her earthenware menagerie. Smiling cats and fish with whimsical expressions were purely decorative, but some of her animal models were also practical. At various times in the 1930s Clarice stated that she thought pottery could be both entertaining and functional, and many of her pieces illustrate these sentiments. A long-legged, thin elephant serves as a napkin ring, a polliwog and a teddy bear are bookends, and a chick is the cocoa pot of a child's drinking set. Sales of such whimsical pieces were never large because of the depressed state of the market, but they remained in production for several years.

Another unusual design Clarice produced in 1932 was *Delecia Citrus,* which revitalized sales of the original *Delecia* style by incorporating hand-painted designs. Bright, stylized oranges and lemons were painted over *Delecia* runnings. Soon *Delecia Citrus* became one of Clarice's best-selling lines.

*Patina,* another new line Clarice created in 1932, was especially imaginative and technically innovative. It required a new process using slip, a clay thinned to the consistency of cream, which literally splattered all over the biscuit ware. When dried, glazed, and fired, the slip gave the flat surface an interesting incrustation. Since it was not possible to outline or band on the surface, because the brush could not follow a regular line, new freehand designs were created to decorate the ware. One design is of a simple tree on a coast, a

*Opposite, above:*
The MARIGOLD design on a thirteen-inch wall plaque, and an ISIS vase. 1931 or 1932.

The FANTASQUE GARDENIA design on an eighteen-inch charger. 1931 or 1932.

*Opposite, below:*
LATONA RED ROSES on a thirteen-inch wall plaque, a 419 bowl, and an ISIS vase. Produced 1930.

A variation of the CAPRICE design on an INSPIRATION thirteen-inch plaque. 1929 or 1930.

British personality Leslie Henson meets Clarice's earthenware menagerie.

Clarice in her studio at Newport Pottery.

second a country landscape, and a third is of a stylized tree with blue foliage.

At about the time *Patina* was being created, Gladys Scarlett, Clarice's first apprentice, resigned. She and Clarice had never talked much, and their relationship did not improve as Clarice became famous and increasingly more distant from the working girls. Gladys's abilities, however, had developed over the years, and she was by now quite a talented decorator. She accepted employment at a competing pottery where she supervised a decorating shop and earned three times the salary she had received at Newport.

Gladys's departure did not slow down production at the *Bizarre* shop, which was employing about 60 decorators plus 130 additional staff members at Wilkinson's involved in the technical and administrative side of producing the ware. Clarice was absorbed in creating new lines, but, rather than producing only ware that she personally found pleasing, she tried to design for every possible taste so as to maximize sales. And as long as she and Colley believed in the sales potential of a new line, nothing stopped it from being produced.

Unfortunately, Colley and Clarice often failed to use good judgment in deciding what to issue. Instead of cautiously producing one or two variations of a new style to test reaction, they went ahead with major production and marketing campaigns for entire new ranges.

One of Clarice's more notable failures was with a range of shapes completely different from anything she had produced previously. Abandoning the geometric forms to which she had been so closely tied, Clarice started designing ware in natural shapes based on tree trunks and branches. The idea was not a new one, such pieces having been produced as early as 1750 in Germany and in the 1800s in Staffordshire. Clarice named her new line *Le Bon Dieu*. She and Colley must have had great faith in the sales potential of the new shapes, because the initial range was large. It included bowls, vases, and a complete tea set.

The publicity statement accompanying the line's release in August 1932 read: "One day a friend gave me a polished wooden block, part of a tree trunk of unusual shape. The moment I saw this an idea came to me to create pottery, taking actual tree trunks as my models." Clarice created her new line by molding clay onto bits of tree trunk.

Sales were disappointing. The dull brown and moss-green shades and the irregular shape of the ware were not accepted by the buying public. Hasty attempts were made to improve its marketability by covering the ware with patterns such as *Nasturtium*. These changes only served to accentuate the ugliness of the basic shape. To many the most appealing feature of *Le Bon Dieu* was the quotation on the base of each piece— "I think that I shall never see, a form as lovely as a tree"—and even this was omitted from the later pieces.

Clarice created *Le Bon Dieu* and her other new lines in time for several major autumn exhibitions. One pattern produced at this time, *Kew*, named after a formal park near London that was stocked with plants from around the world, is simply an adaptation of the *Trees and House* pattern, with the bubble and wedge trees placed on either side of an Oriental building. The design was produced in full on fancy ware and as a shoulder pattern on tableware.

Sales of many of the new lines were disappointing, even though the publicity garnered at the exhibitions was tremendous. More disappointing, however, was another major project that occupied much of Colley's time in 1932 and would cost Clarice much valuable time and productivity in 1933. The project was initiated by none other than the Prince of Wales.

The BIZOOKA on the Newport Pottery float for the 1932 Crazy Day parade, raising funds for local hospitals.

A watercolor illustration from the pattern books of the ORANGE ROOF COTTAGE design. The BIZARRE decorators referred to these pattern books when painting new lines.

BIZOOKA "jockeys" Lily Dabs, Ivy Tunicliff, Rene Dale, and Nancy Flynn.

The vast range of shapes Clarice produced for her LE BON DIEU ware.

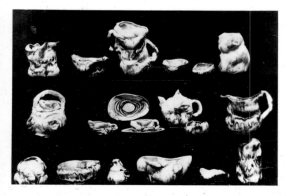

Opposite:
The APPLIQUE LUGANO design on a twelve-inch LOTUS jug, 1930.

# Chapter Eight
## 1933

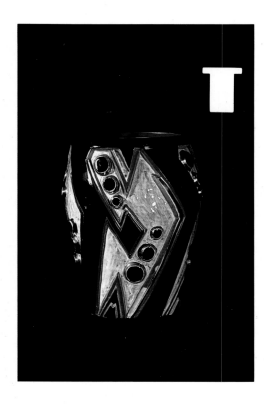

he Prince of Wales had stated in a 1932 speech that British industry "must raise the standard of design of its products, for in design it is outstripped by other countries." A government committee was appointed to encourage manufacturers to use top artists to create designs for British products. For prestige and publicity purposes, their work was to be displayed at exhibitions across the country as well as on tours abroad. In 1933 Cadbury Chocolates, one of the first to respond to the committee's urgings, offered large cash prizes to artists whose designs were accepted for use on their chocolate boxes.

The Potteries' response to this government campaign was to establish its own committee to select top artists to submit designs for production on pottery. On the committee were the top designers of the era and, strangely, Colley Shorter, who was of course not a designer but a businessman. Even stranger, Clarice, who at this time was producing more designs and selling more pottery than any of her competitors, was not invited to join. Nor was Clarice invited to submit designs for review by the committee.

It was agreed by the committee that selected designs would be produced in bone china by the prestigious Brain and Company and in earthenware by Wilkinson's. As art director of Wilkinson's, Clarice had to take charge of this project, a time-consuming activity that she did not relish.

The project turned out to be a disaster. Though some of Britain's most prestigious artists submitted ideas, they showed little understanding of what was needed to produce designs that would innovate pottery production, and none of them even visited Wilkinson's to supervise any stage of production. Clarice was left the task of producing ware far removed from her own ideas. The results, not surprisingly, were poor and caused friction between Clarice and Colley. *Bizarre* girls witnessed several occasions on which Colley shouted at Clarice, much to everyone's embarrassment.

In the summer of 1933 the ware was shown at a major exhibition in London. Albert Rutherston submitted a design with very little decoration that consisted of minute flowers next to loops in gilt. Paul Nash's design was somewhat busier but equally uninspired, consisting of broken lines encircling the object or forming fern shapes. Dod Proctor also resorted to loops in a variety of colors. Vanessa Bell designed an indifferent pattern of leaves and floral shapes in black, blue, and yellow. Even Graham Sutherland, who had helped orchestrate the project, produced a very plain design called *Green Daisy*, which had green spots with stars and loops within a pink band. The most innovative design came from John Armstrong. Called *Chaldean* or *Chevaux*, his piece had a stylized horse in blue and sepia, with a band of brown with stars and lines around it.

**Above left:**
Vase number 470, one of a range of six shapes produced in the SCRAPHITO style. Very few SCRAPHITO pieces were produced, as they did not sell well, but several attempts were made to market them in different colorways. 1930. The handwritten name was spelled SCRAFITO.

**Opposite:**
A CONICAL shape six-person teaset in the SUNBURST design, with, on the third row, a 391 candlestick and a 362 vase. Teapot six inches high.

The critics panned the designs and the public's response was to buy very little of it. Even the fact that the pieces were initially produced in limited-edition sets of twelve did not help sales: John Armstrong's design was the only one to sell in any reasonable quantity. To make matters worse, Colley angered another committee member by including Clarice's name on the backstamp for the new ware, right next to the name of the artist. An attempt was made to salvage the situation when Colley, together with one of the other committee members, invited other artists whom they felt to be more suitable to submit additional designs.

Only one of the twenty-five designers, Frank Brangwyn, displayed his creation in 1933. (The others put on a major exhibition the following year.) The design Brangwyn submitted had originally been commissioned in 1925 to form the main decoration of the Royal Gallery of the House of Lords in London. Unfortunately, the Royal Fine Art Commission considered the design unsuitable but used it in 1934 to decorate a new guildhall in Wales.

Production of Brangwyn's design was on earthenware plaques, and it was a difficult process. The middle section of each plaque is an eight-inch-wide print colored by hand with edges painted freehand. Because of the fine detail, a magnifying glass was needed to apply the large number of colors, which had to be applied in stages so that each was fired at its ideal temperature. This work was done at Wilkinson's.

Although Frank Brangwyn and Clarice were jointly credited in the handwritten mark on the back of the plaques, they were actually painted by Clarice's former mentor, Fred Ridgeway, and Ellen Browne. The plaques were first shown at a major exhibition held in London in October of 1933. They received considerable publicity but, at ten guineas a pair, they were expensive and did not sell well.

When not occupied with preparing for these exhibitions, Clarice found time to produce some of her own designs. These included some of her best landscapes. The curiously named *Secrets* was produced in shades of yellow, brown, and green. Later a *Secrets Orange* was issued with orange banding. Another landscape, *Coral Firs*, was probably inspired by the local Staffordshire hills, which are topped with ragged fir trees. A *Blue Firs* version was also issued. This has several different shades of blue, with red detail.

One of the colors used for *Blue Firs*, number five blue, was difficult to fire successfully because its firing temperature is higher than that of the other colors. Number five blue should ideally have been put on the ware first and fired at 700°, with the other colors then added and fired at 400°. However, with the exception of samples or large pieces of the design, this does not appear to have been done. Much of the ware was fired only at the lower temperature, which caused the blue to fuse improperly to the honeyglaze surface.

The factory was aware of this problem and its people were instructed to pack these pieces with lots of paper to prevent colors from running. Still the factory persisted in producing this faulty ware probably because the design was quite popular. Eventually, when the design was used on a particularly well-selling new tableware shape called *Biarritz*, the use of number five blue was discontinued.

About this same time Clarice produced *Windbells*, which features a black-stemmed tree with lenticular blue foliage against a wavy orange, yellow, and green ground. Some tall, bell-shaped flowers are in the background. *Windbells* was quite popular, selling almost as well as *Coral Firs* and *Secrets*.

Clarice also added a major new range of shapes in 1933, shapes that were inspired by Jean Tetard, the French designer from whom Clarice had copied the idea for her highly successful *Stamford* line. This time, however, Colley paid for the use of Tetard's design ideas up front. The first pieces of this new range of shapes, called *Bon Jour*, coffee and tea sets, were issued in the spring of 1933. They were instantly successful. Large oval *Bon Jour* water jugs were soon issued, and a *Bon Jour* container for jam also appeared. Any item with a lid had a round pastille-shaped knob, echoing the shape it topped. As *Bon Jour* sales continued to increase, *Stamford* was gradually phased out. Although *Conical* ware was still in production at this time, it too was nearing the end of its sales life.

In the summer of 1933 Clarice created new candlesticks for the *Bon Jour* range. Made in flat black pottery with both straight and curved edges, they stand on a pastille-shaped base and have round candle holders attached to flat surfaces at the top. Single-candle and double-candle versions were produced, both most commonly decorated in landscape patterns.

That same summer Clarice added another Tetard shape to her range. The new shape, intended as a tableware version of the *Bon Jour* range, was called *Biarritz*. The plates are oblong with a circular well to hold food, and the tureens are semicircular with a flat, oblong lid. The shapes are impractical because the edges are easily chipped.

*Biarritz* was difficult to manufacture. A round plate is naturally strong and needs little support during firing, but the oblong *Biarritz* ware tended to warp in the kiln. The problem was solved by supporting the ware with sand and special kiln furniture, but this made the ware more expensive to produce, as fewer pieces could be accommodated at each firing.

Despite its high price, *Biarritz* sold well, particularly in North America. The dinner sets were mainly produced in lightly decorated shoulder patterns, with many new designs created specifically for the shape. *Biarritz* plates were also sold individually as wall plaques in patterns such as *Windbells*, *Secrets*, *Blue Firs*, and *Coral Firs*. The range continued in production until 1939.

In the fall of 1933 Clarice supervised the production of yet more new pieces. Working together with the clay department, she produced a new type of clay which, when fired, produced a speckled stoneware body under a clear glaze. She called this finish *Goldstone* and developed many new shapes for it, including heavily ribbed vases, jugs, and tea and coffee sets.

The shapes were very different from the geometric ones she had been so successful with previously: they were designed to look as if they had been thrown on a potter's wheel, and in fact this is how the original model for each was made. Clarice had never learned to throw pots but employed a potter to create shapes under her supervision. Always interested in texture, she particularly enjoyed producing this type of ware.

Since the selling point of these pieces was the finish of the body, Clarice decorated them with small, simple, freehand motifs. They are numbered from approximately 600 upward in the shape catalogue; the name *Lynton* was given to the tea and coffee sets. *Goldstone* did not sell particularly well, but the *Lynton* tea and coffee sets were eventually produced in standard honeyglaze and remained in production for four years.

That fall, Clarice returned to her first love, modeling, and produced one of her smallest pieces—a pie funnel in the shape of a blackbird. Until Clarice designed this blackbird the funnels, necessary to allow the circulation of heat, were simple pottery tubes. She drew her inspiration for the piece from the children's nursery rhyme "Four and twenty blackbirds, baked in a pie," which also gave her a good promotional tool.

An original photograph illustrating shapes in the BON JOUR and BIARRITZ ranges.
This photograph would have been used by salesmen to illustrate the shapes available, which is why the pieces are undecorated.

A stand at an exhibition
full of pieces of GOLDSTONE ware,
primarily produced in shapes
modeled to simulate hand-thrown vases.
The coffee and teasets are in the
LYNTON range.

A selection of ware in the CROCUS design, which was still Clarice's best-selling design in 1933.

The most popular of Clarice's wall masks was called FLORA and was produced in two sizes. Early examples feature more brightly colored flowers; the majority of pieces, however, have the pastel shades typical of the late 1930s.

A MARLENE wall mask, which was in production for several years from 1933 onward.

CHAHAR, this highly modeled mask, was produced in only very small quantities.

The blackbirds were painted underglaze in yellow and black and were very inexpensive to produce. Clarice supervised the production of giant papier-mâché blackbirds and pie-crusts that were distributed for display in store windows for promotional purposes. The blackbirds, which sold for the same price as plain pie-funnels, instantly cornered the market. They continued in production until the 1950s.

Clarice also modeled a number of face masks—or wall medallions, as the factory called them—that were introduced in 1933. The mask called Marlene has an ornate headdress, Flora has an Oriental face decorated with flowers, Marilyn wears a beret, Chahar an elaborate Egyptian headdress, and a pair of baby masks called Jack and Jill wear only smiles beneath their small tufts of hair. There was a good market for such frivolous items, and Marlene and Flora were still in production in the late 1930s.

Less successful was a figure called Night that appeared at the same time. Night, a tall thin woman largely hidden in a long cloak, shows that Clarice's aspirations to be a sculptress were still strong. However, comparison of her attempts at serious sculpting with the amusing trifles she produced shows that she was really only accomplished at the latter.

During the last few months of 1933, Clarice produced some landscape designs with a new style of banding in which a broad pastel band is overlaid with numerous fine lines. *Honolulu* features a tree with a black-and-green-striped trunk and pendulous red, orange, and yellow foliage. The trunk banding shows thin black lines over a broad green band.

*Bridgewater*, introduced at the same time, is banded in yellow with fine mustard lines and features a very finely outlined landscape. The design is one of the most detailed and delicately painted ever to come from the *Bizarre* shop. The last true *Bizarre* landscape, it marks the zenith of *Bizarre* style. Subsequent landscapes were unbanded and lacking in detail. Thus, *Bridgewater* marks the turning point in the *Bizarre* story.

Why the change? Unfortunately, just when the decorators in the *Bizarre* shop had truly perfected their art, market forces dictated its eclipse. Within eighteen months after the production of *Bridgewater*, the majority of ware was being produced without outlining and banding. This style was largely replaced by a painting technique called etching.

Although *Bizarre* ware in its original concept was produced for quite some time after 1933, the stylistic developments of this time marked the eventual disappearance of the word *Bizarre* from the back-stamps. A completely different style of design was to dominate the second half of the 1930s.

A shape 14 vase in the AUREA colorway of the RHODANTHE design.

T he year 1934 was a year of great artistic change for Clarice, as well as a year of frustration. Clarice was often dispirited, depleted, and frustrated because so much of her time was taken up with the production of the designs of other artists, those designers who had been invited by Colley to submit their ideas for a limited-edition series by Britain's industrial design community. Clarice either supervised or personally undertook the production of the designs of twenty-four different artists—an enormous undertaking, especially in view of the fact that many of the artists submitted more than one pattern for the project.

The limited-edition series was unveiled at London's Harrod's department store in December as the culmination of a major campaign to publicize what was obviously intended as a prestigious event. Unfortunately, the publicity campaign was the only part of the event that was successful. Press coverage was extensive but only slightly more positive than before.

Among the better designs on display was the work of Eva Crofts, a textile designer. She exhibited two designs, both on *Bon Jour* early morning sets. One was called *Field Flowers* and shows bright, colorful blooms drawn freehand, very much in the *Bizarre* tradition. The other design shows a couple in medieval costume taking tea.

The most notable work to emerge from the exhibition was Dame Laura Knight's *Circus*. She had already done paintings with circus themes and now transferred this concept to pottery. The plates of her *Circus* dinnerware are decorated in the style of a circus ring. Around the rim is a sea of faces; and in the middle each plate shows a different act: clowns, trapeze artists, performing horses, and a high-wire act. These were produced using a pink outline print, which was then enameled by hand.

Not content with using blanks provided by the factory, she produced an entire range of shapes for her set. The gravy boats have circus performers for the handles. Two chubby clowns, back to back, form the base of a small candlestick. The most impressive piece, however, is a lamp base almost two feet high that has various circus acts balancing precariously, one on top of the other, to form a column. Unfortunately, such style and creativity is expensive to produce, and only a handful of wealthy people were able to pay the seventy pounds for a dinner service for twelve.

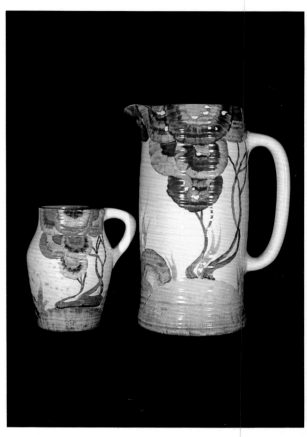

A six-inch jug in the RHODANTHE design and a LYNTON shape jug. Probably 1934 or 1935.

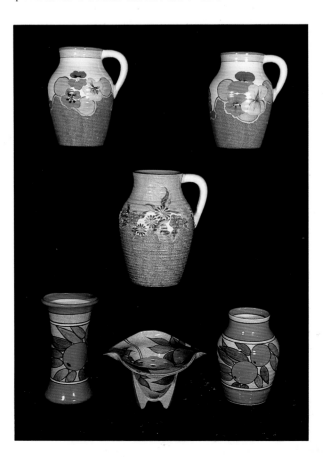

Left:
Top row: a pair of NASTURTIUM ISIS jugs, CANTERBURY BELLS LOTUS jug; bottom row: 205 vase, a 497 vase in ORANGES design with green CAFE-AU-LAIT ground, ISIS vase in ORANGES design.

A TRIESTE shape early morning set decorated in CROCUS.

Part of an exhibition of the Limited Edition series. On the table in the foreground are a Laura Knight dinner- and teaset and a lamp base in her CIRCUS design.

The exhibition of limited-edition pieces toured the country and was eventually taken abroad, but the general reaction of both the press and the public was negative. Wilkinson's undoubtedly lost much money on the series because most of the lines failed to sell in any quantity.

Clarice, who did not submit any designs for the exhibition, nevertheless underwent a profound artistic change during the many months she spent preparing for the exhibition. One can only speculate as to why, but she seemed to have lost the daring that had enabled her to produce such vivid shapes and patterns only a few months earlier. Perhaps taking on this arduous and unpleasant task sapped some of her creativity. Possibly the change in her was a result of maturity, as she was now thirty-five years old. Or maybe the many designers she worked with in preparing the limited-edition series influenced her approach to design, inducing her to become more serious and sedate.

Meanwhile, as Clarice was undergoing her own artistic transformation, the tastes of the buying public were also changing. Although *Bizarre* and *Fantasque* had both become best-sellers in the middle of the Depression, the reduced spending power of the public began to affect the *Bizarre* shop in 1934. Fewer elaborate, purely decorative pieces were ordered, so the factory subsequently placed greater emphasis on the production of functional tableware. One by one the process of outlining, then enameling, then banding was felt to be too expensive, and the factory sought to reduce this type of production.

One range produced by Clarice in response to changing buying habits is called *My Garden*. The ware consists of vases and jugs of simple flowing shapes, decorated with large raised flowers. On some pieces the flower forms the base with a vase rising out of it. On others, the handle of a jug is actually a modeled delphinium. The idea was not entirely new to Clarice, as she had already used modeled flowers as handles for her *Marguerite* ware and on her Flora wall masks.

The bodies of the *My Garden* ware are lightly colored in tan shades over the honeyglaze; the flowers are painted in red, purple, and yellow. The pieces needed no outlining or banding, and it was an easy task for the enamelers to paint the strongly delineated flowers. This was a definite economy for the factory and freed banders for other tasks. *My Garden* proved very popular; it was eventually made with a variety of glazes and sold right up to the end of the 1930s.

The Newport and Wilkinson's office staff in March 1933, when all the office staff were centralized at Wilkinson's. In the back row are Agnes Wordley, cashier Andrew Taylor, Virginia Browe, foreign invoice clerk Vera Bloor, Miss Palmer, and Cyril Hynd (who eventually became a BIZARRE salesman); in the front row, Eric Grindley, Stan Critchlow, and Verdun Stockton.

A publicity shot, probably taken for a sales leaflet, of a range of Clarice's shapes and designs. The many simple patterns for GOLDSTONE is evident, and several of the CONICAL shapes, with the round feet they were eventually given, are shown. The two large vases in the background are MILANO ware, and there are also examples of both single and double BON JOUR candlesticks.

Banders, increasingly freed from producing elaborate designs, were now devoting much of their energy to doing simple banded patterns on tableware. A vast number of new designs consisted only of a variety of bands around the edge of the ware. Outliners were also spending less time on intensive designs and were free to produce the delicate shoulder patterns on the *Biarritz* ware, which needed very little enameling.

Sales of *Biarritz* were very good in 1934, and sales of *Bon Jour* coffee and teaware were even better. When these ranges were first issued, the sets were completed by cups and saucers from the *Conical* series. With increasing sales, however, Clarice felt the need to add matching teaware, particularly for the North American market, which preferred to have everything on the table match. She therefore introduced a new cup and saucer shape that was used both for *Biarritz* and for the *Bon Jour* early morning set. The saucers are oblong in the style of *Biarritz* plates, but the cups have a normal shape with a handle that is a miniature version of the *Bon Jour* teapot handle. Also part of the set are a *Bon Jour* shape creamer and the sugar bowl from the *Stamford* set.

Clarice also adapted some of her *Conical* ware to fit the *Bon Jour* range. The 378 and 379 vases were issued with disk-shaped supports instead of triangular ones, and *Conical* bowls appeared with four disk-shaped feet. A completely new shape combining features of both *Conical* and *Bon Jour* also appeared. Clarice called this *Trieste*. The teapot, creamer, and sugar bowl are shaped like triangles with smooth points, but have flat sides like the *Bon Jour* range. The saucers and plates are three-sided. The set never sold in large quantities, although it was in production for several years.

Another new design introduced in 1934 was named *Rhodanthe*. This typified the move away from the *Bizarre* type of decoration, as it was neither outlined nor banded. Rather, it represents the new style of painting called etching that was to predominate in the second half of the decade. Etching is a form of freehand painting in which, after one color is applied, a second is shaded into it by overlapping the brushstrokes. It is easy to overdo this technique and end up with a khaki color, but the girls quickly learned to do it properly. Etching was used to create the entire *Rhodanthe* design, which is basically a very simple pattern. *Rhodanthe* was immediately successful.

Curiously, 1934 was also the year in which the *Fantasque* mark was gradually phased out. For unknown reasons, pieces that earlier would have been classified as *Fantasque* were now given a new *Bizarre* mark. Although the factory was moving away from the production of *Fantasque* style designs, there remained a definite market for them, and while the name disappeared from the ware during 1934, it continued to be used by the shops and their customers when ordering ware, and the surviving records of Newport Pottery from 1936 still mention *Fantasque*.

Just as *Fantasque* lingered on after its official demise, so did the *Bizarre* style, for in 1934 Clarice introduced new geometric shapes that turned out to be some of her very best—a series of vases for the *Bon Jour* range. The vases are round with flat sides like the *Bon Jour* teapot and were made in single, double, and triple versions, the triple made by joining a single vase to the front of a double. Such vases were difficult to fire; the triple was especially prone to sagging in its middle section. Still Clarice must have persevered in the production of these shapes, as several examples are known and the shapes are featured in advertisements from 1934 and 1935.

The year 1934 was very much a watershed one for Clarice and the Newport Pottery. It was a death knell for the *Bizarre* style and the beginning of a period of profound change in both the fortunes of the factory and in Clarice's artistic style. Her output from this time onward was to be very variable, but there were still many surprises to come.

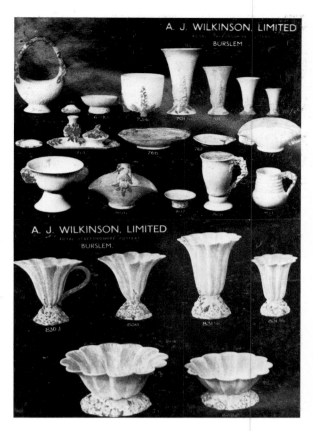

Sales literature for a small part of the MY GARDEN range, which appeared in 1934 and had new shapes added to it in both 1935 and 1936.

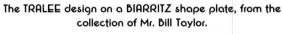

The TRALEE design on a BIARRITZ shape plate, from the collection of Mr. Bill Taylor.

Clarice and Colley (extreme right) pictured with some colleagues after a business meeting.

The KILLARNEY GREEN design on an eight-inch bowl. 1935.

**F**rom 1935 on, change came quickly to Clarice and the *Bizarre* girls. After having been immensely successful for the first half of the decade, Clarice now had to work extremely hard just to maintain her position in the industry. The volume of orders arriving at the factory was decreasing, and any *Bizarre* girl who left was not replaced.

Working in a declining market, Clarice had to be very careful with what she designed. After the debacle with the limited-edition series, the factory could not afford any more failures. The very competitive situation Clarice and Colley faced in both the domestic and overseas markets caused the majority of their output to shift from ornamental pieces to basic tableware. The factory had several hundred tableware designs, each with its own design number, that consisted simply of bands of various color and width combinations. The potential profit was much greater from a dinnerware set produced in a simple banded pattern than from a costly landscape.

Despite this artistically stultifying climate, Clarice was able to produce some pleasing designs in 1935. Playing it safe by using an old standby, she produced some alternate color patterns for *Rhodanthe*, which by this time was established as a strong seller. One predominantly pink version was called *Viscaria*, and a mostly green one *Aurea*.

Clarice then introduced two other designs using the same etching technique as *Rhodanthe*. One, called *Trallee*, has a large, brash cottage and landscape theme. The cottage roof appears thatched because of the etching. On both sides of the cottage tall delphinium flowers among black bushes form a garden. The pattern also includes a blue sky produced in *Cafe-au-Lait* stippling. Two other designs feature a similar scene but with the cottage replaced by a tree. One, in which the delphiniums are blue and pink, is called *Fragrance*. The other, with yellow and orange delphiniums, is *Sandon*, the name derived from the village of Sandon, near Stoke-on-Trent. All three new designs sold reasonably well, but *Trallee* was the most successful.

A new teaware shape that Clarice produced in 1935 is based on the shape of the tropical, spiral-shaped shellfish called nautilus. The teaware has a looped handle and a small open loop on the lid. The design is quite good, but for some reason it was never put into production, although a few trial pieces were sold. The shape was never actually named; we choose to call it *Nautilus*.

WATER LILY ware in various shapes, of which the 973 bowl was the best-seller.

A LYNTON shape ribbed vase, in an abstract design, produced by the INSPIRATION technique. This was made after the actual INSPIRATION ware was discontinued, probably as an experimental piece. 1935.

Opposite:
A twelve-inch-high LYNTON shape vase decorated in the CHERRY BLOSSOM design, 1935.

A contemporary photograph of tableware in the CORNCOB shape. Also visible is a HANDKERCHIEF shape vase.

A later variation in the CONICAL bowl series. The original triangular feet are replaced with pastille-shaped feet. This example is decorated in FOREST GLEN. 1935.

Part of the RAFFIA shape range of ware, from an original photograph.

Further experiments in early 1935 produced some pieces that were executed underglaze rather than on-glaze, as was the practice with typical *Bizarre* ware. An example is *Crayon Scenes*, in which ceramic crayons were used to sketch rural landscapes. These were drawn realistically rather than in a stylized manner and resemble picture postcards in their style and composition. Judging from existing samples, it appears that the designs were produced only on plates. They did not sell well and were soon discontinued.

Clarice and Colley now spent even more time in her studio discussing such failures in a struggle to maintain their position in the market. They would often work together late into the night, taking their only breaks from the factory on weekends.

Clarice had few close friends other than Colley, and because he was a married man, she could only be seen in public with him at the factory and on business trips. Colley did not have much of a home life, as he remained distant from his wife and children. He often spent his weekends drinking at his club. Thus, for both Clarice and Colley, the most meaningful part of their lives was based around the factory. They would continue for several more years to derive significant emotional sustenance only from their work and from their relationship with each other.

The *Bizarre* name was phased out in late 1935: from then on the ware was simply marked "Clarice Cliff." In terms of sheer efficiency this was a sound decision, for very few designs that Clarice had issued before 1935 were produced in the post–*Bizarre* mark days. In theory it was possible to have ordered a 1929 shape with a 1932 pattern in 1936, but few such pieces exist. Occasionally one comes across *Bizarre* ware with the Clarice Cliff mark on it; then it is obvious that it was made after 1935 to replace a broken piece. However, as the second half of the decade progressed and many of the outliners left, it became increasingly difficult to repeat earlier complicated patterns. Matchings of old patterns invariably have thinner colors and differ stylistically from the original because they were not done by the same outliner.

This loss of key personnel was probably one of the reasons the designs changed so radically in 1935. The system of passing the ware from outliner to enameler to bander was disappearing, and many of the new patterns were executed entirely by enamelers.

The first patterns to be introduced after the factory phased out the *Bizarre* mark all seem to have appeared at about the same time, November 1935. Part of the attraction of *Bizarre* and *Fantasque* was the brusqueness with which they were produced, but most of the male decorators had gone by this time, and the more feminine approach is evident in the outline of the post-1935 designs. *Autumn*, for example, often shows great movement in the way it was outlined, but later designs based on a similar composition, such as *Ferndale*, look quite tranquil and peaceful. *Ferndale* resembles *Autumn* in that it has a cluster of trees with low bushes and a cottage on either side, but that is where the similarity ends. The adventurous shades of 1930 are gone:

in *Ferndale*, the ground is brown, the bushes green, the sky blue, and the trees appropriately autumnal.

Although the special *Bizarre* style was now gone, Clarice put to good advantage the delicacy of work the girls in the *Bizarre* shop could now achieve. Her *Brookfields* design, for example, which repeats an earlier motif of a cottage beside a bridge, was produced in realistic greens, yellows, and browns, but Clarice added a little more flair by covering the design from top to bottom in fine blue, yellow, and green bands.

In stark contrast to *Brookfields*, Clarice issued some new designs in 1935 that really were *Bizarre* in the original sense of the word. These are among the last designs issued with the *Bizarre* stamp. Clarice chose the exotic names of *Killarney* and *Sungold* for these patterns. Consisting of a simple geometric design with a star radiating from a central disk and small triangles around the border, they are almost identical to earlier patterns except that thin, translucent, pastel colors replaced thick, blobby enamels. *Killarney* is in shades of green and buff and *Sungold* in yellows. These new designs lack the impact of the original *Bizarre* ware but are nonetheless fitting of the *Bizarre* stamp.

In 1935 Clarice also produced one of her last truly different landscape designs. Called *Forest Glen*, it gives the trees and cottage theme a new dimension. The delicate outline of trees, bushes, and cottage does not jump out immediately; rather, the eye is instantly drawn to a blood-red sky that hangs menacingly over the scene. The sky was applied in the *Delecia* effect, which was used for the last time on this design. Another version of this pattern, identical except for its blue sky, is more rare. Clarice gave this a different name—*Newlyn*.

Most of Clarice's designs of 1936 did not display the same quality of imagination, however. Bright colors, angular shapes, and unusual designs were replaced by conservatively shaped ware decorated in muted shades. Some new lines relied solely on surface ornamentation for their decorative effect. The *Raffia* and *Corncob* shapes are typical of this. Easily and quickly decorated, such designs drastically reduced the cost of producing the ware.

The majority of Clarice's new designs were simple shoulder patterns or motifs for the various tableware shapes that formed the bulk of her output. These consist of several hundred designs, most of which were known only by their pattern number. She did, however, also produce some new landscapes in 1936. *Capri* shows a garden full of trees surrounded by orange and yellow flowers. The entire design is covered in thin concentric lines. *Taormina* has an etched tree in front of a cliff edge and has no banding. *Lorna* is a full landscape with trees, cottage, and bridge, but, because it was produced in natural shades, it lacks the impact of Clarice's earlier landscapes.

Even though the special *Bizarre* magic was now gone from her work, Clarice fulfilled her function as an industrial designer in admirable fashion. She was catering to the tastes of the buying public and making a profit for the factory. Her *My Garden* range continued to sell well, and each shape was now available in four varieties: *Sunrise*, *Verdant*, *Mushroom*, and *Flame*. *Rhodanthe*, *Viscaria*, and *Aurea* were also very successful and led to several other designs with the same etched flowers. One of these, *Morning*, features groups of flowers and thin concentric bands that cover the entire ware. *Honeydew* and *Sundew* feature the same flowers as does *Morning*, but this time fine pastel banding surrounds the edge of the ware.

Around the time Clarice was producing these new lines, several other pottery companies went out of business owing to the depressed state of the market and their failure to adequately adapt. Thanks to Clarice, however, 1936 was a good year for Newport and Wilkinson's. The Clarice Cliff name was still selling impressive amounts of pottery.

Examples of the NAUTILUS shape teaware that were never put into full production.

## Chapter Eleven
## 1937 to 1941

In 1937 Clarice and Colley, in order to keep the business afloat, had to gear their output to the demands of the buying public, emphasizing conservatively decorated tableware. Still business remained poor. Until the salesmen returned with their orders on Saturday, it was not known what the girls would be decorating the following week.

The demand for *Bizarre*-style ware had disappeared almost completely, and the few landscapes introduced by Clarice in 1937 were her last. One of these, a design called *Clovelly*, shows some vestiges of the old *Bizarre* style. It is a coastal landscape with tall trees, houses hidden among bushes, and, in the distance, a view of the sea with a small island. Other landscapes include *Chalet*, a delicately drawn building in the middle of a cottage garden overflowing with flowers. *Napoli* is also done very delicately, covering only a small part of the ware. It features a garden fountain with gold stars in the sky above; most were produced on a mushroom glaze background. *Stile and Trees* shows a set of steps and a fence surrounded by trees. None of these designs was produced in any great quantity, and their low sales proved that the market for such ware was gone.

Some of the designs from earlier years were still being produced in modified form on tableware. *Coral Firs, Blue Firs*, and *Secrets*, were occasionally ordered on *Biarritz* sets as late as 1938. *Crocus* and *Rhodanthe* continued to be popular, and Clarice introduced lithographs featuring flowers or scenes. These were typical of the ware that would predominate after the war.

Several new glazes were introduced in 1937, including a bright apple green, but the most successful was the mushroom glaze. This has a matte finish and is seen on many shapes, serving as the entire decoration on some and forming a background on others.

Also in 1937, Clarice produced her *Windsor* range. The tea- and coffeepot are basically pear shaped, with ill-matching handles that have small blades to strengthen them where they join the body. The *Windsor* shape sold quite well and is generally found only in lightly decorated patterns.

While producing *Windsor*, Clarice also adapted *Lynton* shape teaware to form a new line called *Gnome Nursery* ware. The handles on the pieces are small green gnomes; the body has just a plain, honeyglaze finish. This sold only moderately well.

Sales improved slightly in 1938 with the introduction of a series of ware meant to resemble water lilies floating on water. The range is large, including teaware and various dishes, and the first pieces issued had shape numbers in the high 900s. A new number series was started with later pieces numbered from 100 upwards. The water-lily bowl, number 973, was a good seller, both before and after the war. The bowl was inexpensive to produce and easy to decorate, as the girls simply had to paint the raised shapes.

Also introduced in 1938 was the *Harvest* range, which features raised motifs of corn sheaves and bunches of fruit. It is covered in a strikingly yellow honeyglaze with just touches of paint on the fruit and sold well both before and after the war.

Less successful was a range of earthenware horoscope signs; each sign was produced in relief on a star-shaped base. Also unsuccessful was a series of ashtrays: one a hippopotamus that holds a cigarette in its mouth; another a dove that holds a cigarette between its tail feathers. There was little market for such novelties.

In terms of business output the year 1939 was uneventful until September 3. On that day Great Britain entered World War II. All British industries were profoundly affected, and the Potteries were no exception.

The War Office swung quickly into action to determine what resources were available, ordering all pottery manufacturers to take inventory and report available stock. Subsequently, Colley was able to sell to the government at full market price ware that had been held in the Wilkinson's warehouses for twenty or thirty years. This was a boon to the faltering factory.

In the first few months of the war, production was switched to essential tableware and other ware for the troops. Soon, however, key staff members from all departments were drafted into the military, and production began to decrease. The few remaining decorators continued hand-painting for a short time to fill orders that had been placed prior to the outbreak of war.

It was about this time that Colley's wife died. Annie Shorter had been chronically ill for much of her married life and had spent the year prior to her death confined to a hospital. It was a quiet funeral, which Clarice did not attend.

Back at the factory, the *Bizarre* shop was closed down in compliance with government regulations, and the staff transferred from Newport to Wilkinson's. The decorators immediately called their new room the *New Bizarre* shop. The few *Bizarre* girls who were left continued in employment despite government restrictions on the amount of decorated ware that could be produced. Some of the shapes with embossed designs that had been introduced just before the war, such as *Harvest*, were issued without painted detail, mainly for export. Clarice and the *Bizarre* girls helped in other departments, all of which were short-staffed. The girls also aided the war effort by knitting items for the soldiers during their breaks.

During this period, Clarice spent most of her spare time with Colley; the two were virtually inseparable since Annie's death. On December 21, 1940, Clarice and Colley were secretly married.

They kept their marriage a secret for almost a full year. Perhaps since they were still separated by class they felt that neither would be accepted by the other's family, or perhaps Colley felt uncomfortable about remarrying so soon after Annie's death. For whatever reason, it was not until November 1941 that they began to tell their families of the union.

In the winter of 1941 they took a belated honeymoon in Wales, where Clarice met some of Colley's family. Neither the bride's nor the groom's family were pleased about the marriage, and few of them ever visited Colley and Clarice at their home. The couple, however, seemed unperturbed by this situation and settled down to a quiet life at Colley's estate as Britain fought a war that, in 1941, showed no sign of ending.

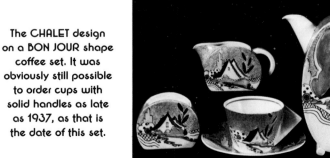

The CHALET design on a BON JOUR shape coffee set. It was obviously still possible to order cups with solid handles as late as 1937, as that is the date of this set.

A DAFFODIL shape bowl (450) and a candlestick in the NAPOLI design on a mushroom glaze.

# Chapter Twelve
## 1941 to 1964

It was obvious that the war would be a long one and all British industries faced the problems of lack of skilled workers, lack of materials, and the need to deal with a mass of government regulations. The Board of Trade was especially onerous. It required that the Potteries give priority to ware produced for export and reduce decorated earthenware production to one-fifth of its prewar level. Wilkinson's therefore produced mainly export ware or purely practical goods to be used both by the troops and by the British public.

Clarice Cliff-Shorter, as she now called herself, spent much of her time at her new home with Colley. Because of increasing government restrictions, there was little demand at the factory for her artistic talents. By 1942 no further decorated ware could be produced for domestic use. Restrictions were also imposed on the number of shapes that could be made; only plain, white, undecorated utility ware was free of quotas.

These restrictions were only partially lifted when the war ended in 1945. It was to be some years before it became permissible to make decorated ware for domestic consumption, so the production of such ware for export became Colley's priority. Thus designs were dictated mainly by the tastes of overseas buyers, with North America the main market. Unfortunately, the North American preference was mainly for mundane, conservatively shaped ware. In response to this, the factory produced traditional designs with lithographs and prints with hand-painted detail. This gave little impetus for Clarice to design, but by now she had become accustomed to being a housewife, tending her garden, and looking after Colley, who was now sixty-three.

Clarice did manage to produce a handful of new designs during the postwar years, but all of them are quite mundane. Her *Georgian* shape, for example, features a raised dental edge and no decoration other than simple banding, either blue and gold or green and gold. The shape range is extensive, including tea, coffee, and dinner sets. It was also issued with lithographs of traditional prints, many of them based on nineteenth-century designs.

Orders were still arriving for *Crocus*, which was now produced in pastel shades as well as in its original style. Occasionally Clarice would ask for prewar patterns on her new shapes. *Rhodanthe* was produced briefly, and some trial pieces with *Delecia* runnings were made, but there proved to be no demand for them.

The dominance of the overseas market is reflected in the style of back-stamps used on the ware after World War II. Although Clarice's facsimile signature was still on each piece, more elaborate markings surrounded it, and emphasis was now placed on the phrase "Royal Staffordshire Ceramics," which helped to sell the ware abroad.

By 1950 Clarice was spending so little time at the factory that an assistant art director was hired—Eric Elliot, recruited from the Burslem School of Art. Eric shared with Clarice a studio that contained drawers full of material about the limited-edition ware made in the 1930s. When he compared this and some random pieces of the old *Bizarre* ware with that which the factory was presently producing, he realized how uninspired the latter was. This may have spurred him to produce some bold, floral patterns of the style that Clarice had issued some fifteen years back. Among these was *Magnolia*, which features a bold white-and-pink flower; because Eric's designs were all issued with Clarice Cliff markings, he cleverly worked his own initials into the design of the floral leaves. Another bold design he produced was *Paris*, which has a similar floral motif, this time on a solid black background. *Magnolia* was completely hand-painted by the new *Bizarre* girls, but *Paris* used an outline print with painted detail.

One of the most innovative shapes to appear from the factory after the war was designed by neither Eric

nor Clarice. The *Tepee* teapot was created by Betty Silvester, who had originally worked as a decorator in the *Bizarre* shop in the late 1930s. Designed specifically for the Canadian market, the teapot is in the shape of a tepee with an Indian brave for the spout and a totem pole for the handle. Unfortunately, Betty Silvester was not credited with the design; it has just a Clarice Cliff mark and "Greetings from Canada" on the base. Betty had many ideas for new shapes, as evidenced by her drawings that still exist in old pattern books, but very few were ever produced.

In 1952 all restrictions on the production of decorated ware were lifted. Colley decided to take advantage of this by producing wares to commemorate the coronation of Queen Elizabeth II. He anticipated a good market for such designs both in Britain and abroad. What was produced, however, was simply a lithograph of the queen's official picture on *Georgian*-shape tableware. A process involving electric engraving was used to reproduce the queen's likeness in sharp sepia tones amid a band of heraldic devices. These were printed and then enameled by hand. The process was expensive, because the engraving quickly wore out and had to be replaced. The ware sold well in Canada, however. The pieces' elaborate back-stamp reads, "Confederation Series Canada, Approved by the Council of Industrial Design, Clarice Cliff, Royal Staffordshire Ceramics, Burslem, England."

A more imaginative series of ware was designed by Eric Elliot in 1954. Called *Sunkissed*, it features lemons, pears, and cucumbers. It was produced using a vague black print outline that the girls then painted. The *Sunkissed* line represents the nearest the factory came after the war to producing ware in the *Bizarre* style. Unfortunately, Eric left the factory shortly after this. Both Clarice and Colley were sad to see him go.

Eric was not replaced. Neither Colley nor Clarice felt the need for a contemporary designer, as they were not trying to compete with those potteries producing contemporary shapes and designs. Also, neither Colley nor Clarice was in the best of health. They both smoked heavily, and Clarice was overweight. Her once jet-black hair was now white. By 1960 Colley was seventy-eight years old, and, though he still worked a full schedule, his failing health and advanced years undoubtedly kept him from running the factory with his former efficiency.

Other pottery manufacturers were issuing new streamlined shapes and designs, but Wilkinson's was having problems just producing its traditional wares. Sales declined rapidly; by 1960 overseas sales were the lowest they had been in ten years. Domestic sales also suffered, owing in part to a 30 percent sales tax that had been initiated in 1955.

To add to their troubles, Colley was hospitalized in 1961. For the next several years Clarice spent all her time taking care of him. Finally, in 1963 at the age of eighty-one, he died. Clarice was grief-stricken. Colley had been her best friend and her husband, and now she was alone.

Clarice inherited the factory where she had spent a lifetime. With the fire and intensity she possessed during her *Bizarre* years she might very well have been able to resuscitate the ailing business, but now she was a sixty-four-year-old, lonely woman in poor health. She decided to sell the factory to Midwinter's, a competing Pottery. The negotiations with Midwinter's and the transfer of ownership took many months to finalize. But one day in the winter of 1964, the sale was completed. At Clarice's insistence, any of the staff who wanted to stay on were permitted to do so. Clarice's job was done, and the last tie was broken with the place in which she had risen from apprentice girl to designer, and then art director. She left the Pottery, no longer hers, and was never to return.

CLARICE CLIFF DESIGNS "CANADA" SOUVENIR TEAPOT FOR TOURIST TR

A Canadian wholesaler advertisement for the TEEPEE teapot, designed by M. B. Silvester

## Chapter Thirteen
## 1964 to 1972

Throughout the 1960s a growing band of collectors sought out anything dating from the 1930s: furniture, rugs, old radios, glass, chrome, and pottery. Particularly prized were brightly colored items with brash designs. They searched second-hand shops and flea markets for pieces and soon came across pottery with intriguing names such as *Bizarre* and *Fantasque*. These pieces could be bought very inexpensively, because few people saw them as being anything but junk. It was not long, however, before increasing interest developed in the art of the 1930s. Authors, who were often also collectors, began to research and write about it.

The first author to write exclusively about the Art Deco era was Bevis Hillier, who said, "Of all materials, ceramics were the least well adapted to Art Deco. Hard-edged materials like silver lent themselves to cubist design but pottery, fluid and malleable, did not." Hillier was obviously unaware of the shapes produced by Clarice Cliff.

In 1969 Martin Battersby published *Decorative Thirties*, in which, having done a thorough job of researching the artists and designers of the era, he gained the distinction of being the first writer to reassemble the cast that had orchestrated British pottery design in the 1930s. His well-chosen illustrations spurred many collectors to seek out the work of Clarice Cliff. Indeed, he had the vision to list in his book all the British designers whose work would be in the greatest demand fifteen years later.

Clarice, in poor health and living virtually in seclusion, was oblivious to the growing enthusiasm about her work. Researchers who obtained her telephone number were told politely but firmly that the records of her work had been destroyed and that it was impossible for her to help them.

Perhaps she slowed down the growing excitement about her art, but she could not stop it. Astute dealers in central London knew a good thing when they saw it and were amazed by the variety of shapes and designs Clarice had produced. As competition among dealers grew, their costs rose and the prices to their customers increased. To be sure, many in the antiques trade failed to understand the attraction of the wares; antiques periodicals largely ignored the interest in Clarice and in Art Deco in general. But this served to limit the number of outlets carrying the ware, and so competition and prices continued to rise.

The *Bizarre* ware archives that Clarice had believed no longer existed were, in fact, almost destroyed in 1969. The disused office in which they had lain was scheduled for demolition to allow new construction at Wilkinson's. Many of the large books and files were ruined by water from the leaky roof. Fortunately, someone called in the staff from Stoke-on-Trent Museum and Library to save items of importance. It was easy for them to decide what to take: they simply chose the items that had not been ruined by the weather. They recovered a large cross section of materials, but entire books full of details about *Bizarre* and Clarice were lost when the building was destroyed shortly afterward.

In 1971 Bevis Hillier was instrumental in organizing an exhibition called the "World of Art Deco" at the Minneapolis Institute of Arts in Minnesota. Hillier made up for omitting Clarice's work from his *Art Deco* book by including thirty-two lots of *Bizarre* pottery in the ceramics section.

In 1972 Martin Battersby played a major role in setting up the first museum exhibition of Clarice's pottery in Great Britain, held at the Brighton Museum in Sussex. The museum curator, wanting some background information on the pottery and the person who designed it, telephoned Clarice personally. Clarice was surprised that anyone should take such interest in her work but was impressed by the enthusiasm the organizers had for it. Therefore, in addition to writing a brief account of the *Bizarre* years for the catalogue, she also contributed notes on the exhibits and loaned some pieces from her own collection.

More than a hundred pieces from the *Bizarre* years were put on display at the museum. Clarice herself did not attend the exhibition, but the notes she contributed to the catalogue gave collectors important information about the origins of her art. The fact that a working-class girl had been capable of achieving such a position and producing such startling pottery made them all the more interested in her work. Explanations about its production as well as Clarice's other comments in the catalogue served to build up the mystique already attached to her, inspiring even more people to become collectors.

Sadly, Clarice's catalogue notes also indicate that she must have been ill when she wrote them. She remembered very few of the design names, even forgetting the name of the *Stamford* teapot, and omitted mention of Colley's role in her success.

Some months after the exhibition closed, Clarice died, quietly succumbing to heart failure. Although 1972 marked the end of Clarice's life, it was the beginning of an era in which the interest and publicity sparked by her *Bizarre* ware would be even greater than when it had first appeared, forty-four years earlier. If Clarice was surprised toward the end of her life that anyone should show interest in the products of the *Bizarre* era, she would have been astounded at how that interest would mushroom in the coming years.

Clarice Cliff in the 1960s.

**Part of the Brighton Museum Clarice Cliff exhibition in 1972.**
(Photograph courtesy of Brighton Museum and Art Gallery)

Colley Shorter
pictured in the 1940s.

# Epilogue
# 1972 to 1987

**T**he pottery industry in which Clarice had worked for over fifty years had never formally acknowledged her talent, but in the years following her death the seemingly endless range of Clarice's shapes and designs that kept appearing in auctions and antique fairs captured the interest of myriad collectors. Many skeptical dealers believed that this interest would be only temporary, and several ceramic historians expressed a dislike for her work; but among collectors Clarice was soon regarded as the most important ceramic designer of her generation. She had produced so many unusual designs and shapes in such large quantities that the scope for collectors was enormous. None of Clarice's contemporaries had been so prolific, and so their pieces attracted fewer collectors.

As prices for Clarice's pottery rose, samples of her work began to appear at prestigious auctions. In 1974 a Forest Glen charger became the first piece to sell for more than a hundred pounds. Still, new collectors could pick up pieces cheaply, since most antiques dealers had little knowledge of her work.

In 1976 two enthusiastic Clarice Cliff collectors, Peter Wentworth-Shields and Kay Johnson, wrote a small book titled *Clarice Cliff*. It briefly told her life story but lacked the scope to name and date her huge range of designs and shapes. It did, however, further stimulate interest in her work, and as a result prices continued to rise. During 1977 and 1978, tea and coffee sets began to sell at London auction houses for about one hundred pounds.

Authors writing about the 1930s or Art Deco either criticized or completely ignored Clarice's work. The 1979 exhibition "Thirties" at the Hayward Gallery in London was also guilty of largely ignoring Clarice's contribution to British ceramics. They chose to exhibit only one *Inspiration* vase but displayed many pieces from the limited-edition series. Since these had sold very poorly when first issued, their inclusion in the exhibit seems to demonstrate questionable judgment. Indeed, with the exception of the Frank Brangwyn and Dame Laura Knight pieces, this series has proven to be of little interest to collectors. Most of the pieces are obtainable at a price that, when adjusted for inflation, is less than they were sold for originally. In contrast, prices for Clarice's ware continued to rise dramatically along with the enthusiasm of collectors. Having employed sixty decorators for over ten years, Clarice had produced so much pottery that upon its rediscovery it quickly dominated the collecting market.

In 1981 I decided to form the Clarice Cliff Collectors Club. Having collected her work since 1978, I had become frustrated at the lack of information on both Clarice and her pottery. My intention was to build up an extensive photographic archive of pieces from members' collections and also to research the answers to the many questions the pottery presented. I quickly realized that the best source of information would be the *Bizarre* girls themselves, and set about finding them. My task was difficult because most of them had married and changed their names, but I was able to trace Gladys Scarlett, and in the following three years I found more than twenty others.

By 1983 interest in Clarice's pottery was such that Christie's organized an auction of 160 of her pieces. Collectors from around the world vied with each other, and once again record prices were set. Unfortunately, the auction catalogue, which was later marketed as a reference work, was filled with errors, providing incorrect names and production dates for many of her designs. Collectors still did not have a reliable source of information about their pieces.

In 1984, a chance phone call between Louis Meisel and myself made us realize that we shared similar aims. We both wanted to produce the definitive book on Clarice Cliff, and the best way to do that was to combine our information and resources.

My research continued, as did Louis's, and I spent many hours at the Midwinter factory going through the *Bizarre* shop and a nearby tip composed of thousands of broken pieces of *Bizarre* ware. Midwinter's management asked my advice on the production of a set of limited-edition reproduction pieces of Clarice's work. Also advising them was Ethel Barrow, one of the original *Bizarre* girls and the first decorator responsible for doing the *Crocus* design. She demonstrated for us her execution of the brushstrokes; we watched spellbound as she decorated pieces at a speed we found amazing, but which she thought slow.

It took Midwinter's over a year to reproduce four shapes—a shape 14 vase in *Honolulu*, a *Conical* bowl in *Umbrellas* and *Rain*, a *Summerhouse* thirteen-inch plaque, and a set of six *Conical* sugar sifters—while the people working under Clarice in the 1930s produced dozens of new shapes every year. Midwinter's also issued lithograph versions of *Oranges & Lemons*, *Crocus*, and *Melon*. These pieces appeared in retail outlets that had first stocked Clarice's designs fifty-seven years earlier. The limited-edition pieces sold out with amazing speed. Clarice had been paid the compliment of having her shapes and designs reproduced for a new generation, a generation eager to own a piece of her innovative work.

The ultimate accolade came when Clarice's life and works were featured in a four-part television series. Her wares dominated the screen and spurred even more people to collect her work. The art of hand-painting had all but disappeared, but now, in a sense, it was being brought back to life. Clarice Cliff would have been pleased.

The *Bizarre* years were like a ceramic rainbow. They seemed to have appeared from nowhere, dazzled with their color, and quickly faded. The rediscovery of Clarice's work, however, has proven that the *Bizarre* designs and shapes were very much ahead of their time and now are here to stay. Unlike the rainbow, the richness of Clarice's work, the wealth of designs and forms that she bequeathed to us, will not fade.

Sherds of BIZARRE ware unearthed opposite the old Newport Pottery factory by Leonard Griffin in March 1984.

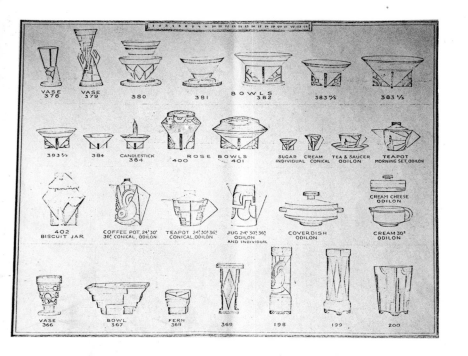

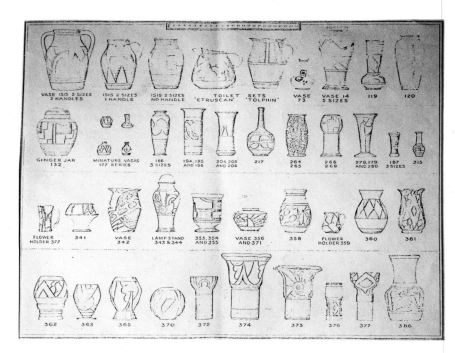

## SHAPE NUMBERS AND NAMES

It is extremely difficult to categorize factories' output of shapes. Some shapes were given numbers, some names, and some had both. Further, many shapes introduced by Wilkinson's and Newport between 1919 and 1928 were later utilized by Clarice for *Bizarre* ware. In some cases these shapes retained their original shape number, while others were allocated a new one. For example, the Girl Candlestick, which first appeared in 1925, was given shape number 431, which is part of the number sequence used in 1930. Therefore, although as a general rule the higher a shape number is, the later the piece appeared, there are some exceptions.

Many of the shapes Clarice used were produced in several sizes. Vase shape numbers 194, 195, and 196 are three different sizes of the same shape. However, another vase in three different sizes was classified under one shape number, 186. Sometimes vases of the same shape but different sizes were not numbered sequentially; for example, a ribbed globular vase was numbered both 356 and 371. Occasionally the same number was accidentally used twice—377 was both a flower holder and an *Archaic* vase shape. Shape numbers after 341 seem to have been designed by Clarice, or under her supervision, from 1929 onward. Most of the shapes between 220 and 340 were probably also her work, and many of them were used for *Bizarre* production. Pre-1928 shapes that were reintroduced with new shape numbers seem to include 411, 412, 414, 415, and 425–31. These were all figurines or figurines adapted to form bookends.

Shape numbers were assigned as new shapes were introduced. Since examples cannot be found for every number, it appears that either not all numbers were allocated, or some were given to shapes that never actually appeared in the shops. Shape names were also used erratically by the factory. The *Lotus* jug, which Clarice used many times for her designs, had initially been produced as part of a jug and bowl set in 1919. From then until 1929 many pieces actually had the words "Lotus Shape" molded in the base. However, in the literature produced after 1929 the factory referred to them as *Isis* jugs, and this name was then molded in the base. To avoid confusion we have referred to this shape by its original name, which seems to be the one most used by collectors. Similarly, when the tea and coffee shapes of the *Conical* series were launched they were referred to as being of *Odilon* shape. Again, we have chosen the more obvious name.

Many shapes were marketed in dual roles, and so were referred to by more than one name in the factories' literature and press releases. The Chicken Teapot was also called a Chicken Cocoa Pot when it was used as part of a child's set. The Hen and Chick cruet set was also called a "Cock-a-doodle-do" set. The small *Conical* bowl 384 was sold as both a sugar bowl and a slop bowl. Particular problems are found in the terminology used for the *Bon Jour/Biarritz* shapes. The oblong plates were called *Biarritz*, the oblong saucers *Bon Jour*. Similarly an *Odilon* sauce boat and a *Stamford* vegetable dish were but variations on the same shape.

The confusion in the number and name classification reflects how busy the factories were in the period. Luckily, some of the original sheets supplied to the salesmen and stockers of the ware have survived, and these cover the majority of the important shapes produced. A look at these sheets, while remembering that each of the shapes could have been ordered with any of Clarice's range of designs gives one an idea of the tremendous variety offered.

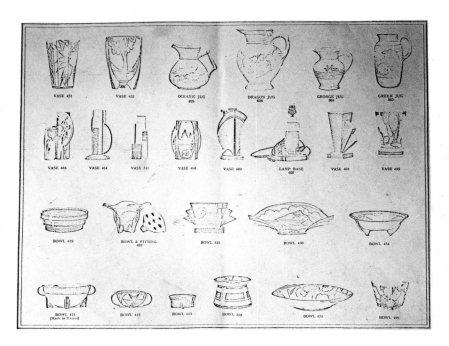

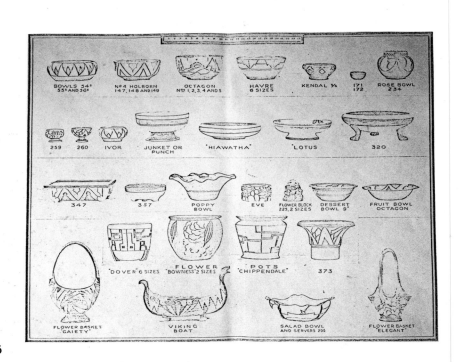

## Chronological Sequence of Shape Numbers and Names

Reference to the list and to the shape sheets allows the ware to be dated with reasonable accuracy. However, as is the case with designs they only show the date *after* which the shape was available. The first date a shape appeared can sometimes be ascertained exactly, but in some cases the first and last numbers of each year are estimated. Quite a few of the more popular shapes were in production for several years after they were introduced.

**1919**
*Lotus* jug patented by Wilkinson's
**1921—26**
Numbers 16 through 220 known to have been in production
**1924—25**
Clarice's handmade figures
**1925**
Girl Candlestick and *Apple Honey* shapes introduced
**1927**
Numbers 221 to 280 introduced
**September 1927**
*Viking Boat* shape
**1928**
Numbers 281 to 340 introduced

**1929**
Numbers 341 to 402 introduced
**April 1929**
*Archaic* shapes 372 to 377
**June 1929**
*Conical* shapes 378 to 384
**September 1929**
*Conical* teaware

**1930**
Numbers 403 to 449 introduced
**September 1930**
*Age of Jazz* figures 432 to 436 *Stamford* teapot
**1931**
Numbers 450 to 499 introduced

**September 1931**
*Conical* sugar dredger 489
**1932**
Numbers 500 to 590 introduced
**August 1932**
*Le Bon Dieu* shapes 562, 573 to 577, and 589

**1933**
Numbers 591 to 630 introduced
**March 1933**
First *Bon Jour/Biarritz* shapes
**1934**
Numbers 631 to 680 introduced
**July 1934**
First *My Garden* series 660 to 672

**1935**
Numbers 681 to 720 introduced
Second *My Garden* series 701
**1936**
Numbers 721 to 835 introduced
Third *My Garden* series 806 to 832
**1937**
Numbers 836 to 920 introduced
*Harvest* ware 900 to 915 (approximate)
**1938—39**
Numbers 920 to 999 and New series introduced
Shape numbers from 100 on

## Notes on the A. J. Wilkinson Shape Sheet

Although produced in the same format, these sheets very likely date from different times. The ones with bowls and vases of low shape numbers seem to have been produced in 1930; the vase shapes illustrated between 14 and 315 are the only ones still in regular production by 1930. Early shapes other than these in *Bizarre* patterns are known but are quite rare. Some of the early shapes were still in production in 1935. The sheet with vases and bowls in the 400 and 500 series probably dates from 1932, although many of the shapes appeared originally in 1931. Some of the sheets combine shapes produced in the 1930s with ones from the 1920s that were reintroduced after the success of *Bizarre*.

Shape 512, refers to the *Stamford* tea and hot water set, and was not the shape number of the *Stamford* teapot. Indeed, like most tea and coffee ware this piece was not assigned a shape number.

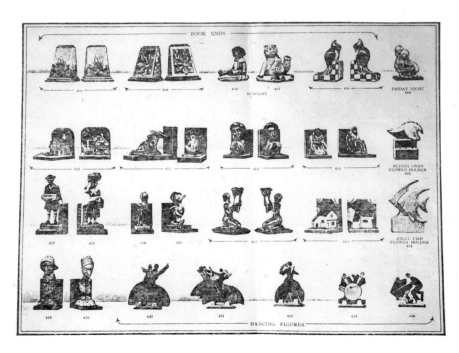

A demonstration at James Colmer's Store in Bath February 1936. Nancy Dale is decorating a LOTUS jug, and Lily Barrow is banding a vase in CORAL FIRS.

# CATALOGUE OF THE DECORATORS

Although the *"Bizarre* girls" formed the majority of Clarice's decorators, the boys who were recruited straight from art school in 1928 and 1929 actually did most of the outlining in the late 1920s and early 1930s. Harold Walker and John Shaw were the two most important boys, working on the largest pieces of ware and specials. Fred Salmon and Tom Stringer outlined the smaller pieces and tableware; both left by 1933.

The most important girl outliner in the early years of the *Bizarre* shop was Ellen Browne, who was a very talented artist; Ella Hopkins, Annie Beresford, Kathy Keeling, and Eileen Tharme also outlined for part of this time. Because the quality of the outlining was a critical aspect of the ware, few decorators were entrusted to do this.

Only girls in the *Bizarre* shop were enamelers, who applied the colors within the outlines previously painted. Most of these girls were also freehand painters, and would apply patterns with no outline, such as *Crocus*, *Gayday*, and *Rhodanthe*. Because most of the girls were able both to enamel and to paint freehand, they have been listed simply as enamelers.

The third group of decorators in the *Bizarre* shop, the banders and liners, were also all girls. They applied thick bands or thin lines of color by spinning ware on a wheel by hand. In the early years most of their work was banding the previously outlined and enameled patterns, but after 1935 many of the designs had no banding, so they concentrated on producing tableware with simple banded patterns in numerous colors.

The vast majority of the decorators were employed between 1928 and 1930. There were more than sixty *Bizarre* girls in the early 1930s, but by the end of the decade there were only about forty. The boys had all left by 1936, and the style of ware produced after this date changes noticeably.

Clarice's policy was to assign a certain decorator to each design, from samples through completed orders. This ensured that each piece in a range was produced in the same style. Only when a design became extremely popular would another decorator also produce it, to keep up with demand. Comparison of many pieces of *Secrets*, *Trees and House*, and *Coral Firs*, for example, reveals stylistic differences between them, and it is possible to recognize which pieces were painted by the same decorator.

Most pieces had no decorator's mark. When a mark is found, however, it can sometimes disclose the identity of the decorator. Generally, in the early 1930s marks were only used when more than one decorator produced the same pattern at the same time. Then one or both would mark the piece with an initial, or sometimes a simple symbol, to distinguish their work, and to enable calculation of their piecework payments. On mass-produced patterns such as *Crocus*, *Ravel*, and *Secrets* the mark may be that of a team who produced the piece. The color of the mark offers a clue as to whether it is that of the outliner, the enameler, or the bander. If it is in a color not on the actual design, it is unlikely to be a decorator's mark but was probably put on to ensure that it went to a certain salesman or to indicate that it was for a particular exhibition. In addition, since marks were often changed and many of the decorators had the same initial and had to resort to a symbol, no mark is conclusive proof of a decorator's identity. However, the same mark on different pieces of ware does show that the same person decorated those pieces.

Not included in this listing is Lily Slater, who did not actually work on specific pieces. All the *Bizarre* girls emphasize the important role Lily played in producing the ware, however. Initially a painter herself at Newport, shortly after *Bizarre* was launched she became the missus of the shop. She trained the inexperienced girls who joined the staff, helped in the execution of complicated patterns, and allocated ware for decoration.

Hilda Lovatt also played a role in Clarice's success as her assistant. She was not greatly involved in the day-to-day running of the *Bizarre* shop but helped Clarice in many ways, and on the many occasions when Clarice was away, she ensured that her wishes were being followed.

In order not to complicate the listing, in nearly every case the maiden name of the *Bizarre* girls has been used, since most were unmarried when they joined the shop.

The BIZARRE girls practicing first aid at the start of World War II. Left to right they are Mollie Browne, Ella Hopkins, Doreen Yates, Eileen Tharme, Winnie Pound, and Edna Cheetham.

Clarice's hand-painted dedication on one of the plates of the dinner service she presented to Hilda Grindley in 1938.

...y a BIZARRE wedding: Marjory Higginson's wedding ...y in June of 1940, where all but one of the female ...uests were fellow painters from the BIZARRE shop. On Marjory's left is her sister Dorothy.

Ethel Barrow, the original CROCUS girl, demonstrating the brushstrokes used to produce the flowers with which she has been associated since 1928.

BIZARRE girl Mary Brown demonstrating banding at an exhibition in 1929.

Leonard Griffin with Mary Brown in 1985.

**ALICE ANDREWS**
1930 to 1942 and briefly in 1946. An enameler who specialized in retouching paint of ware that had been rubbed in the kiln, Alice became missus of the *Bizarre* shop when Lily Slater left.

**GLADYS BAGGALEY**
1932 to 1935.

**DORIS BAILEY**
1929 to 1939. An enameler.

**ETHEL BARROW**
1926 to 1938 and 1948 to 1964. Worked at Wilkinson's before moving to Clarice in 1928 specifically to do *Crocus*. With its immediate success she became responsible for showing many other painters how to execute the brushstrokes, and occasionally did other patterns.

**LILY BARROW**
1930 to 1938. The sister of Ethel Barrow, she decorated *Delecia, Crocus,* and *Nasturtium,* and also went on many demonstrations.

**EDNA BECKET**
1926 to 1939. Initially at Wilkinson's, Edna joined the *Bizarre* shop in 1928 and did the stippling on *Cafe-au-Lait,* enameled *Gibraltar,* and did the semicircles on the floral *Inspiration* designs.

**DORIS BEECH**
1928 to 1932. Joined from the Burslem School of Art with John Shaw and Harold Walker.

**ANNIE BERESFORD**
1926 to 1934. An outliner taken by Clarice from her sister Dolly's shop in 1928.

**GLADYS BIRKIN**
1930 to 1940. An outliner.

**MAY BOOTH**
1937 to 1939. An enameler.

**LAURA BOSSONS**
1929 to 1935. An enameler.

**CLARA BRINDLEY**
1933 to 1939. A bander.

**MARY BROWN**
1925 to 1938 and 1956 to 1965. A bander and liner taken by Clarice from her sister Dolly's shop. One of Clarice's longest-serving employees, she banded many of the designs produced and went on numerous demonstrations. Around 1933 she was transferred briefly to work with Ethel Cliff decorating majolica at Shorter's factory in Stoke.

**ELLEN BROWNE**
July 1928 to July 1940. The most versatile of Clarice's female outliners. Joined from the Burslem School of Art and did the outlining on most of the *Inspiration* ware, *Trees and House,* and later worked on the *Brangwyn* plaques and the *Circus* ware of Dame Laura Knight.

**MOLLIE BROWNE**
October 1932 to July 1940. The younger sister of Ellen, Mollie was a bander and liner and also did the runnings on some later *Delecia.*

**EDNA CHEETHAM**
1934 to March 1941. Decorated *Crocus, Rhodanthe,* and the blackbird pie-funnels.

**ETHEL CLIFF**
1930 to 1940s. Clarice's sister, she joined from Adam's of Tunstall. Worked as a painter for Clarice and at Shorter's majolica factory.

**ETHEL COATES**
1929 to 1939. An enameler.

**ADA CORNES**
1928 to 1940. An enameler.

**ANNIE COTTON**
1928 to 1940. An enameler.

**LILY DABBS**
1932. The younger sister of Nora Dabbs, she worked in the *Bizarre* shop only briefly.

**NORA DABBS**
1930 to 1943. A gilder at Wilkinson's before joining Clarice as a bander and liner, she worked on *Gayday* and *Delecia* and also went on several demonstrations.

**BETTY DAKIN**
1929 to 1934. An enameler.

**NANCY DALE**
1929 to 1939. An enameler.

**RENE DALE**
1931 to 1941 and 1945 to 1953. An enameler initially, painting *Crocus* and *Gayday,* René eventually outlined designs such as *Secrets.* Her mark was an "R" or a dash.

**PEGGY DAVIES**
1936 to 1939. Recruited by Clarice and Colley from the Burslem School of Art, Peggy was unhappy at Newport but was held to her apprentice contract for three years, during which time Clarice used some of her designs. Peggy later joined Doulton's, where she became one of their most important postwar modelers.

**WINNIE DAVIES**
1928 to about 1940. Joined from Wilkinson's, where she was a gilder. A bander and liner, Winnie also worked on *Delecia.*

**ELSIE DEVON**
Joined Dolly Cliff from Adam's of Tunstall and then moved to the *Bizarre* shop in 1930 as an enameler.

**AGNES DURBER**
1928 to 1941. An enameler.

**FLORRIE EARDLEY**
1929 to 1939. An enameler.

**ANNIE ELSBY**
1929 to 1939. An enameler.

**BETH EVANS**
1929 to 1950. A bander and liner, Beth did many patterns including the brown on *Crocus* and *Gayday.*

**VIOLET FARLEY**
1929 to 1939. An enameler.

**NANCY FLYNN**
Early 1930s. Nancy worked only briefly in the *Bizarre* shop.

**NANCY GREATREX**
Late 1930s. Nancy worked only briefly in the *Bizarre* shop.

**NELLIE HARRISON**
1928 to 1930. One of the first girls to work with Clarice before *Bizarre* ware appeared, a bander, but also the one to whom Clarice turned if she wanted anything out of the ordinary produced.

**BETTY HENSHALL**
1929 to 1939. An enameler.

**DOROTHY HIGGINSON**
1930 to 1939. An enameler, Marjory Higginson's sister.

**MARJORY HIGGINSON**
1928 to 1941 and 1952 to 1958. An enameler who worked on various lines including *Inspiration, Trees and House,* and *Delecia,* and also did many demonstrations.

**CONNIE HODGKINSON**
1935 to 1938. An enameler who worked on *Crocus.*

**PHOEBE HODGKINSON**
1929 to 1938. Initially worked in Newport's number 10 shop with Lily Slater. Worked for Clarice as an enameler on *Applique* and doing decoration that required fine detail. Also decorated sample plaques and vases. Her mark was dot, dash, dot.

**ANNIE HOLLAND**
1930 to 1937. An enameler.

Betty Dakin in 1933, a year before she died.

Beth Evans pictured near the factory in the summer of 1933.

Marjory Higginson relaxing at Westcliff-on-Sea.

May Keeling in 1984. She did not paint the FOREST GLEN plate she is holding, but examples of her work at another pottery can be seen on the shelf behind her.

DELECIA enameler Elsie Nixon in 1985.

A toast to the BIZARRE years, in very rare CHARLOTTE READ tea cups, by Cissie Rhodes, Phyllis Woodhead, and Vera Rawlinson in 1985. Phyllis decorated the CHARLOTTE READ plaque on the wall in 1946.

## ELLA HOPKINS
1929 to 1939. An outliner who produced many patterns for Clarice until she left to work for Wedgwood's.

## KATIE HULME
1933 to 1941. A bander and liner.

## ANNIE JACKSON
1929 to 1940. A bander and liner.

## DORIS JOHNSON
1934 to 1940. An enameler who decorated *Rhodanthe*, *Nasturtium*, and *Honeydew*. Her mark was two dots.

## MAUD JONES
1929 to 1932. A Wilkinson's gilder who worked for Clarice as a bander and liner.

## ELSIE KEARNS
1932 to 1941. A bander.

## MAY KEELING
1928 to 1932. An enameler who worked on *Applique* and *Crocus*.

## KATHY KEELING
1928 to 1940. An outliner.

## NANCY LAWTON
A Wilkinson's gilder who joined the *Bizarre* shop in 1929.

## MILLIE LIVERSAGE
Nancy's older sister, who worked briefly in the *Bizarre* shop.

## NANCY LIVERSAGE
1928 to 1940s. Worked with Clarice at Wilkinson's until joining the *Bizarre* shop. Unlike most of the *Bizarre* girls, Nancy was "day waged," as she spent much time painting matchings. Her mark may have been an "N".

## GERTY LOVE
1928 to 1939. An enameler who painted *Gayday*.

## SADIE MASKREY
1929 to 1933. An enameler who decorated many lines and samples, including *Applique Lugano* and *Inspiration* ware.

## JESSIE McKENZIE
1930 to 1935. An enameler.

## MARY MOSES
1928 to 1941 and 1948 to 1952. An enameler. Her mark was an "M".

## ELSIE NIXON
1929 to 1939. An enameler who worked on *Delecia* and *Gayday*, Elsie also developed the photographs Clarice took in her studio.

## VERA PARR
1934 to 1930. An enameler.

## HILDA PEERS
1929 to 1930. An enameler. Before joining Clarice she worked at Adam's of Tunstall and, briefly, with Dolly Cliff.

## EDITH POINTON
1930s. An enameler who worked briefly in the *Bizarre* shop.

## WINNIE POUND
1930 to 1941 and 1945 to 1947. An enameler who worked on various designs including *Crocus*, on which she wrote the word "Crocus" in green until the stamp was introduced.

## VERA RAWLINSON
1928 to 1929. Taken from Wilkinson's by Clarice prior to the launch of *Bizarre* ware, Vera decorated the *Original Bizarre*.

## CISSIE RHODES
1928 to 1939 and 1949 to 1968. Having started at Wilkinson's in 1926, Cissie Rhodes, an enameler, became the longest-serving *Bizarre* girl.

## HARRIET RHODES
1929 to early 1930s. Joined from Adam's of Tunstall as a bander and liner. No relation to Cissie Rhodes.

## AUDREY RIDGEWAY
Early 1930s. A daughter of Fred Ridgeway who worked briefly in the *Bizarre* shop.

## BERYL RIDGEWAY
Early 1930s. A daughter of Fred Ridgeway who worked briefly in the *Bizarre* shop.

## FRED RIDGEWAY
Not one of Clarice's decorators as such, Fred was a designer she worked under before her success. A very gifted artist who was employed by the factory to work on the highest quality lines, pieces for shows, and such items as the *Brangwyn* plaques, Fred appears to have worked on ware with Clarice Cliff markings throughout most of the 1930s.

## ROSA RIGBY
Early 1930s. A bander and liner from Wilkinson's.

## FLORRIE ROBINSON
1930 to 1937. An enameler.

## FRED SALMON
September 1929 to March 1932. The last of the boy outliners to join Clarice. Came from the Newcastle Art school and decorated *Broth* and other early *Fantasque* designs, mainly the smaller pieces and teasets. Occasionally Clarice used his designs as the basis for a new pattern.

## GLADYS SCARLETT
1928 to 1932. The first decorator to work with Clarice, chosen by Colley Shorter from Dolly Cliff's shop at Wilkinson's. She initially outlined the designs that led to the *Original Bizarre*, and as the designs became more complicated she did banding and lining.

## DAISY SECKERCON
Late 1920s to early 1930s. An enameler.

## JOHN SHAW
1928 to 1936. Joined from the Burslem School of Art with Harold Walker and Tom Stringer in 1928. In addition to being one of the main outliners, he also did some designing, but it is not known which, if any, of his designs Clarice used. He and Harold Walker, the last remaining two boy decorators, left to go into business together.

## PATTY SHAW
Mid-1930s. An enameler who decorated several lines, including the Joan Shorter children's ware. Not related to John Shaw.

## WINNIE SMITH
A bander and liner who joined in 1929.

## IVY STRINGER
1929 to 1941. Moved to Wilkinson's from Newport's number 10 shop and from there to the *Bizarre* shop, where he worked on *Inspiration*, *Crocus*, *Gayday*, and drew the freehand flowers on *Delecia Poppy*.

## TOM STRINGER
1928 to 1933. Joined from the Burslem School of Art in 1928 with Harold Walker and John Shaw and outlined *Broth* and *Autumn*.

## NELLIE THACKER
1928 to late 1930s. Moved from Wilkinson's to work for Clarice as an enameler.

## EILEEN THARME
1928 to 1941. The younger of the Tharme sisters, worked as an outliner on numerous patterns including the *Fantasque* landscapes, *Applique*, *Chintz*, and *Latona*. When there were no orders for these she painted *Crocus*. Her mark was an "E"

Outliner Fred Salmon holding a BROTH plate, one of the pieces he decorated.

Elsie Nixon at Westcliff-on-Sea.

Eileen Tharme (left) and Marjory Higginson on holiday in Scarborough in 1934.

Sisters Ellen and Phyllis Tharme in 1983.

On board the "Newport Pottery Skool" float in 1931 are: front row, Elsie Nixon, unknown, unknown, Mary Brown, Ellen Browne, and Elsie Devon; back row, Sadie Maskrey, Nancy Dale (in dunce cap), Winnie Smith, Nellie Thacker, and Eileen Tharme.

**PHYLLIS THARME**
1928 to 1939. The sixth person to join the *Bizarre* shop, where she banded and lined, working mainly on *Crocus*.

**DORIS THIRLWALL**
1930 to 1936. A bander and liner.

**CLARA THOMAS**
1928 to 1959. The first girl to join Clarice as a bander and liner before *Bizarre* was launched. She was with Dolly Cliff prior to this.

**ETHEL TIMMIS**
1932 to 1937. An enameler who painted *Honeydew*, *Aurea*, blackbird pie-funnels, and other pieces.

**LUCY TRAVIS**
1928 to 1936. An enameler.

**IVY TUNICLIFF**
1932 to 1939. A bander and liner.

**HAROLD WALKER**
1928 to 1936. One of the major boy outliners from the Burs-lem School of Art, entrusted with specials. Some of his designs are detailed in the pattern books, but actual examples are not known. He spent much of his time outlining. Left with John Shaw in 1936.

**EDITH WALTON**
Early 1930s. Worked briefly in the *Bizarre* shop.

**NELLIE WEBB**
August 1928 to 1941. An enameler who worked on *My Garden* ware during the mid-1930s.

**FLORRIE WINKLE**
1928 to 1934. One of the first girls to work with Clarice, an enameler.

**PHYLLIS WOODHEAD**
Mid-1928 to 1932. Initially enameled *Original Bizarre*, then *Broth*, and then *Crocus* before leaving with May Keeling in 1932.

**DOREEN YATES**
1933 to 1940. An enameler.

BIZARRE outliner Harold Walker, pictured at age sixteen in 1928, with his pet bird.

Reg Lamb, who worked for Clarice from 1919 until her death, first as her clay maker, then as her gardener.

The last of the BIZARRE girls hand-painting CROCUS ware in 1961. Cissie Rhodes is on the left, and next to her is Ethel Barrow. Just out of the picture is Mary Brown, the only other BIZARRE girl left at the time.

The BIZARRE shop in 1930. Behind the ware yet to be enameled and banded are: on the first bench, Kathy Keeling, Gerty Love, and Winnie Smith; on the second bench, May Keeling, Nellie Thacker, Harold Walker, and Tom Stringer; on the third bench, Cissie Rhodes, an unknown painter, Ellen Browne, and Fred Salmon; in the fourth row, Vera Hollins and John Shaw (far right).

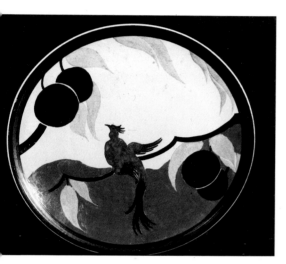

The Edouard Benedictus butterfly design on which Clarice based her BUTTERFLY pattern.

# A TO Z OF CLARICE CLIFF'S DESIGNS

The listing includes only those designs issued between 1928 and 1941. Titles of designs not given a name, or for which the original name is not known, are listed in quotation marks.

The factory was not always consistent with use of names, and there are some variations between the printed literature and the actual names used by the staff. For example, *Taormina* was shortened to *Tamena* by the salesmen. Some press releases, which the factory issued voluminously, also wrongly named designs. In most cases original design names used in this listing have been verified by more than one source. However, it appears that some very popular early designs were never named but ordered by number, or in some cases, as the extant order books show, by a drawing of the design sent by the shop with the order.

Colorways of designs were often specified by adding the dominant color to the design name here again the name used varied. *Orange Autumn* was often also called *Autumn Orange*. For ease of reference the design name will normally precede the colorway, except in those examples where the color has nearly always preceded the design, such as *Blue Firs* and *Coral Firs*.

In some cases the referents of the original design names are unknown. The names are included in this list to help future clarification.

Many names referred either to a type of glaze, or a design produced by a unique method. These include *Applique, Delecia, Gloria, Latona, Nuage, Patina, Persian,* and *Inspiration*. They are included here for ease of reference and the designs produced in each range are listed after.

Production dates for designs produced by hand-painting can only be accurate for the date first introduced. Some ware was produced in very small quantities over several years, other designs were produced in large quantities over a brief time span. All of Clarice's designs could be ordered at any time, however, and "matchings" of any pattern were always available. Certain painters specialized in producing these, and examples of 1930 designs are known on ware produced as late as 1939.

Designs exported from Britain tended to be the gaudier ones, and these would therefore often still be in production for overseas buyers when they were no longer being ordered on the home market. This again makes it difficult to state when a particular design finished regular production. However, the vast majority of Clarice's designs were in production for a year or less.

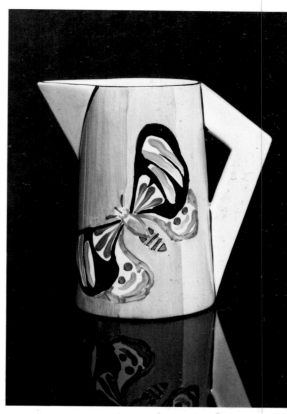

Clarice's BUTTERFLY pattern on a CONICAL jug.

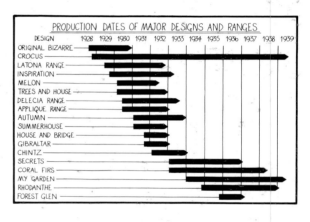

PRODUCTION DATES OF MAJOR DESIGNS AND RANGES

| DESIGN | 1928 | 1929 | 1930 | 1931 | 1932 | 1933 | 1934 | 1935 | 1936 | 1937 | 1938 | 1939 |
|---|---|---|---|---|---|---|---|---|---|---|---|---|
| ORIGINAL BIZARRE | | | | | | | | | | | | |
| CROCUS | | | | | | | | | | | | |
| LATONA RANGE | | | | | | | | | | | | |
| INSPIRATION | | | | | | | | | | | | |
| MELON | | | | | | | | | | | | |
| TREES AND HOUSE | | | | | | | | | | | | |
| DELECIA RANGE | | | | | | | | | | | | |
| APPLIQUE RANGE | | | | | | | | | | | | |
| AUTUMN | | | | | | | | | | | | |
| SUMMERHOUSE | | | | | | | | | | | | |
| HOUSE AND BRIDGE | | | | | | | | | | | | |
| GIBRALTAR | | | | | | | | | | | | |
| CHINTZ | | | | | | | | | | | | |
| SECRETS | | | | | | | | | | | | |
| CORAL FIRS | | | | | | | | | | | | |
| MY GARDEN | | | | | | | | | | | | |
| RHODANTHE | | | | | | | | | | | | |
| FOREST GLEN | | | | | | | | | | | | |

The APPLIQUE BIRD OF PARADISE design on a thirteen-inch plaque.

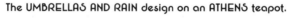

The UMBRELLAS AND RAIN design on an ATHENS teapot.

The MOWCOP design on WINDSOR shape ware.

The CAPRICE design as drawn in the Newport Pottery pattern book.

The CABBAGE FLOWER design on a BIARRITZ plate.

The Da Silva Bruhn carpet design copied by Clarice.

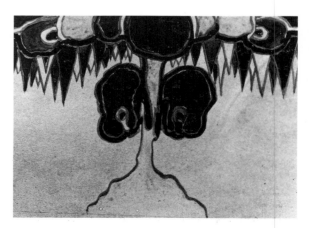

The original KANDINA design from the pattern book.

# A

### ACACIA
No known examples of this pattern, which had a large tree next to a small one. Produced briefly in 1932.

### ALTON
Inspired by Alton Towers, a large ornamental park to the east of Stoke, this had two towers rising from stylized trees, bushes, and flowers. Most common is *Alton Green*; also produced was *Alton Brown*. Production probably during both 1933 and 1934.

### AMBER ROSE
Red and yellow roses with green foliage painted freehand, no outline. Produced briefly 1933 or 1934.

### ANEMONE
Flowers painted realistically, generally on a mushroom-glazed piece of ware, such as the *Book Vases* produced in the late 1930s. Only a partial decoration.

### APPLES
Stylized apples and grapes in natural colors, but with pink, yellow, and orange leaves, and black oblongs resembling piano notes. Produced briefly in 1931 and 1932.

### APPLIQUE
A range produced using a concentrated form of the hand-painting technique. With little or no outline, the design was produced using allover color. Only in later examples was part of the honeyglaze left unpainted. *Applique* was more expensive than *Bizarre* and *Fantasque*, as it used more colors. Banding took three forms: black/honeyglaze, black/red/black, and black/red/black/yellow. The first *Applique* was issued in 1930, the last in 1933, but examples were probably produced for some years afterward. Several of the designs listed are only known from one or two examples, and these may have never gone beyond the sample stage.

### APPLIQUE LUCERNE
A mountainous landscape, with a castle on a hilltop, and the battlements of another castle in the foreground. Slight color variations: *Lucerne Orange* with orange sky and blue castle roofs, *Lucerne Blue* with blue sky and orange castle roofs. One of the first two *Applique* designs, introduced in 1930, but some examples known from as late as 1933.

### APPLIQUE LUGANO
Very similar to *Lucerne* but with a watermill instead of a castle. As before, *Lugano Orange* and *Lugano Blue*. This and *Lucerne* were both directly copied from designs produced by Edouard Benedictus that Clarice had purchased in London. Introduced at same time as *Lucerne*.

### APPLIQUE AVIGNON
Stylistically similar to *Applique Lucerne* and *Lugano*, this featured a bridge in an ornamental garden. Produced six months after the first two designs, it does not appear to been done in any colorway except with an orange sky. Production probably limited to 1930 and 1931.

### APPLIQUE PALERMO
In the foreground a climbing floral plant, in the background a bay sweeps round with two red-sailed yachts on the sea; unlike the first three *Applique* designs the sky is left plain. 1930 to 1931.

### APPLIQUE "RED TREE"
A highly stylised landscape with a red tree with green, orange, and yellow hills and a gray sky. 1930.

### APPLIQUE "WINDMILL"
A blue windmill next to a blue river, with some bushes. Very few examples known, dating from 1930 to 1931.

### APPLIQUE "CARAVAN"
A gypsy caravan under trees laden with red and orange fruit. Few examples, dates from 1931.

### APPLIQUE BIRD OF PARADISE
A yellow and red bird sitting on the branch of a cherry tree with big black fruit. 1931.

### APPLIQUE BLOSSOM
Red, yellow, and blue flowers against a checkered orange background. Very rare. 1931.

### APPLIQUE IDYLL
A cottage garden, with a lady wearing a crinoline dress in the foreground under a fruit tree. Sometimes she is reaching up into the tree. Very unlike the rest of the *Applique* series, as it is produced in pastel colors and pastel banding instead of the black/red/yellow *Applique* banding. It may have been made part of the series simply to use up the supply of *Applique* marks the factory had. Probably introduced in 1932, to go with other manufacturers' successful treatments of a Crinoline lady.

### ARCHAIC
A series of vases modeled as classical pillars. Clarice produced this series under Colley's guidance, and the designs and shapes were copied from *The Grammar of Ornament* by Owen Jones, which dated from 1856. Produced only briefly in 1929, but the vase shapes were utilized with later designs.

### ARIZONA
A mid-1930s tableware pattern featuring an abstract semicircular motif and thin parallel lines.

### AUREA
The third and rarest colorway of the *Rhodanthe* design. Dominantly green, produced 1935 to 1937.

### AUTUMN
Trees with sinuous stems and balloon-shaped foliage and a cottage half-hidden by bushes. Numerous colorways produced, the earliest, *Red Autumn*, dating from 1931. The majority of the designs were produced in the *Blue Autumn* colorway, also in 1931, in which the tree was colored blue, green, and yellow. *Orange Autumn* was dominantly orange and yellow and dates from 1932, as does *Pastel Autumn*, issued in shades of pink, green, and blue. Variations and matchings of the basic design were issued sporadically for several years.

### AWAKENING
A name from a 1932 order book, the design unknown.

# B

### BEECHWOOD
A creamy matte glaze, with a partial decoration of a twig with some leaves, in shades of brown. Produced only briefly in 1936.

### BERRIES
Red and orange berries, blue and purple leaves, with green and yellow oblongs either side. *Fantasque* pattern 1930 to 1931.

### BIGNOU
A partial pattern on dinner and teaware. A sunburst in green, orange, and yellow, on triangular cup handles, and as a segment on the side of plates. 1930.

### BIZARRE
Not the name of any particular design, but used as an overall title for the first geometric patterns. These can be differentiated from the later geometrics by their cruder paintwork and brasher colors. First pieces just had "Bizarre" painted on the back until the large *Bizarre* mark was introduced. Despite being the design that really made Clarice a success, it was only produced in its original form between 1928 and 1930. Production was switched to the more sophisticated geometrics and landscapes eighteen months after *Bizarre* was launched. Large quantities of it were produced, however, in almost all cases on the nongeometric shapes. By the 1930s orders referred to this as *Original Bizarre*, which seems a sensible name to use.

### BLOSSOM
See *Applique*.

### BLUE CHINTZ
Stylized water-lily leaves and buds in blue, green, and pink, in a design giving an effect of a fabric. A very popular design produced in 1932, 1933, and later. An orange colorway was also a good seller, and *Green Chintz* is known from a few examples.

### BLUE CROCUS
See *Crocus*.

### "BLUE DAISY"
A floral abstract with a daisy-shaped flower, between a grid of lines, all painted freehand. Early 1930s.

### BLUE FIRS
A landscape with tall, straggly fir trees in the foreground, and a bleak plain behind. Some examples have part of a cliff and the roof of a house. This was the rarer colorway of *Coral Firs* and dates from 1933. It was only produced in small quantities due to problems involved in firing the number five blue colour from which it took its name.

### BLUE JAPAN
A mottled blue sky and mottled brown ground, with a summerhouse in the background and a tree in the foreground. A very delicately painted pattern, produced briefly in 1933.

### BLUE MEDALLION
A name from the 1932 order book, design not known.

### BLUE RIBBON
A floral design, with a ribbon running among the flowers. Very limited production in 1932.

### "BLUE W"
An abstract design in bright orange, yellow, blue, and green. 1929 or 1930.

### BROOKFIELD
A 1936 landscape, with a delicately painted cottage next to a bridge and a plowed field in the background. The whole design covered in fine blue and yellow banding. Possibly named after a village in Scotland, near Glasgow. Only produced briefly.

### BRIDGEWATER
A river with reeds, a tree shaped like a question mark beside it, and in the background a pair of cottages. Two colorways: in one the tree has orange and red foliage, in the other green. Produced briefly in 1934.

### BROTH
*Fantasque* 105 originally, given a name when it sold well. Bubbles and cobwebs interwoven. One colorway with dominant orange, the other with dominant red. 1929 to 1930.

### "BUTTERFLY"
A crudely painted butterfly on a rough background of striped orange, yellow, and brown. A design copied from Edouard Benedictus. 1930.

# C

### "CABBAGE FLOWER"
A freehand floral pattern, roughly painted green flower, with brown swirl-shaped ground under it. Produced briefly in 1934.

### CAERLEON
Unknown design from 1932.

### CAFE-AU-LAIT
A range in which the dominant feature is a stipple effect, giving the ware an overall color dominance, upon which was added a floral or fruit motif. Also, some standard patterns such as *Autumn* and *Summerhouse* were produced utilizing this effect. Pieces marked *Cafe-au-Lait* produced 1931 to 1933. However, the technique was also used on other patterns, such as *Blue Japan* and *Tralee*.

### CANTERBURY BELLS
Stylized floral pattern, previously (wrongly) attributed to the *Solomon's Seal* pattern. 1932 to 1933.

### CAPRI
A garden with bushes and trees in natural colors, above a block of solid color, the whole covered in fine bands. Two colorways, *Capri Orange* and *Capri Green* produced in 1933 and 1934.

### CAPRICE
A landscape with several trees against an undecorated background. Produced on gray glaze. Production probably limited to 1929 and 1930. This design was also used for the *Inspiration* series.

### "CARPET"
Pattern copied by Clarice from an illustration in a magazine of a carpet designed by Da Silva Bruhn. Curved lines and dots in red, gray, and black. 1930 only.

### CHALET
A garden scene with colorful flower beds leading up a path to a chalet-style building, against a mottled *Cafe-au-Lait* sky. One of the last landscapes, this was produced briefly in 1936 and 1937.

### CHERRY
*Fantasque* pattern 102 originally, part of the first *Fantasque* range introduced in 1929. A blue outline with purple and jade colored berries and leaves and orange detail. Only produced briefly.

### CHERRY BLOSSOM
A design where the ware is covered in green and deep red *Delecia*-style runnings, over which is painted branches with small round white blossoms produced by rubbing a clear circle in the wet paint with a finger tip, and the middle of the flower was then painted in. 1935.

### CHESTNUT
Leaves in relief, colored in natural shades. A range of shapes were produced in this style, the bodies of a dull mushroom-colored glaze. 1938.

### CHRISTINE
A plain tableware pattern, produced by a mixture of print and

hand-painting techniques. A small floral motif in the center of the ware, with hatching around the rim. Produced briefly in 1934 in blue and brown colorways.

### CITRUS

See *Delecia*.

### CLEMATIS

A tableware pattern from the late 1930s of stylized clematis flowers.

### CLOUVRE

A pattern from the *Inspiration* range, given its own design name. Produced by a mixture of *Inspiration* glaze and hand-painting techniques, part of the ware was left without the deep blue glaze, and after firing was then painted with brash, stylized flowers in bright colors and fired again. 1930.

### CLOVELLY

The last seascape pattern produced. Red-roofed houses leading to the sea, in which is a small island; the scene was completed with tall trees and seagulls. Both a shoulder pattern for tableware and a fully decorated version of this design are known. Issued briefly in 1937, it was Newport pattern number 6932.

### "COMETS"

An early abstract pattern. Interwoven comet shapes, with small floral motifs at their head, produced in green, orange, blue, and yellow with black outline. 1930.

### CORAL FIRS

A best-selling landscape pattern introduced in 1933. Initially a full landscape with fir trees, a plain, cliffs, and the roof of a house, it was reduced by 1935 to a shoulder pattern for tableware and continued to sell well. *Blue Firs* and *Green Firs* alternate colorways.

### CRAYON SCENES

Limited to plates, this was a set of six scenes produced with ceramic crayons on biscuit ware, which was then glazed and fired. All designs were realistic and naturalistically colored. Discontinued quickly due to lack of sales. 1934.

### CREPE DE CHINE

A pale green glaze with green and yellow flowers within a black outline, produced briefly in 1933.

### CROCUS

The best-selling pattern, introduced in 1928, and, with the exception of the war years in production until 1963. Initially, the demand was so great that a special *Crocus* shop was formed under the *Bizarre* shop with fifteen to twenty girls painting only this pattern. By the mid-1930s sales declined and it was produced in the *Bizarre* shop. Numerous colorways, and the design was also used on various glazes.

### ORIGINAL CROCUS

The most common version. Flowers in orange, blue, and purple, banding in tan and yellow.

### SPRING CROCUS

Flowers in pastel shades of pink, yellow, and blue. Introduced in the 1930s and variations in production until 1963. After the war pieces simply marked *Crocus*.

### BLUE CROCUS

Flowers in several shades of blue, produced briefly in the middle of the 1930s.

### PETER PAN CROCUS

A black print of a tree and landscape in silhouette, with hand-painted flowers around the tree's base.

### GLORIA CROCUS

Crocus flowers used as an underglaze decoration. See *Gloria*.

### "CUBES"

An abstract design with overlapping colored cubes. 1929 or 1930.

## D

### DAMASK ROSE

A pink glaze, upon which various floral motifs were painted. The quality of the glaze itself was the main selling point, as obtaining an even color over all the ware was quite a technical achievement. Introduced in late 1931 and discontinued by the end of 1932.

### DELECIA

A range with a decoration of runnings produced by mixing raw color with turps and allowing this to run over the ware. When first introduced the effect was put all over the ware, using various colors. The painters were encouraged to experiment, and each piece is different. Introduced in 1930, and produced for about 18 months.

### DELECIA CITRUS

Orange and yellow fruit with green and gray runnings under them. Introduced in 1932. A rare version of this has the fruit colored in silver and gold luster finish.

### DELECIA DAISY/POPPY/PANSY

Each features the appropriate flower with colorful runnings underneath. All the versions were produced only in small quantities and date from 1933 and 1934.

### DEVON

See *Moonlight*.

### "DIAMONDS"

A design featuring two panels, one with a diamond-shaped motif, the other with an abstract one, decorated in yellow, orange, and blue. 1929 or 1930.

### DIJON

A design name from the 1936 order book, pattern unknown.

### DOLPHINS

A tableware pattern with a band of dolphins around the edge of the ware, painted in red.

### DORE

An oblong with an abstract design and a floral motif over one side. Printed outline, with hand-painted color. Produced exclusively for Harrod's in the early 1930s.

### DRYDAY

A lightly decorated landscape with a tree and small fried-egg-shaped flowers around it, produced on a mushroom glaze, it is unusual in that it uses white, which is quite rare. Late 1930s, very limited production.

## E

### EXOTIC

A tableware pattern from the late 1930s, with leaves and gold lines painted as a shoulder motif.

## F

### FANTASQUE

Not a design name, but the name of a range. The success of *Bizarre* ware, which was credited to Newport Pottery for tax purposes even though it was part of Wilkinson's, led Colley Shorter to issue this range with Wilkinson's credited as the manufacturer. This continued through 1930, but by 1931 *Fantasque* was credited to Newport, and *Bizarre* was credited to both factories, which must have totally confused the tax authorities. However, with very few exceptions, all *Bizarre* and *Fantasque* ware was produced in the decorating shops at Newport. *Fantasque* was introduced in late 1929 and discontinued in 1934. *Fantasque* designs theoretically were available, however, until the war, so can be found with just *Bizarre* or Clarice Cliff markings.

### FARMHOUSE

A cottage with a ground-to-roof-level chimney stack in a garden full of trees and bushes, in black, brown, orange, and green. In the foreground are bushes indicated only by outline, with flowers in them. First issued in 1931.

### FERNDALE

A mid-1930s landscape with a tree and a cottage and bushes in the background. May be named after a small village near Mountain Ash in the Welsh Valleys. Very limited production.

### FLORA (1)

A shoulder pattern with an outline print of stylized flower buds, colored by hand in blue and orange. Produced in 1930 on tea sets and tableware.

### FLORA (2)

A wall mask featuring a woman's face surrounded with flowers. Early versions in honeyglaze, later in mushroom glaze, small and large sizes. 1933 to 1937.

### "FLOWER AND SQUARES"

Overlapping squares, with a stylized orange daisy between some of them. 1929 or 1930.

### FLOWER MUSIC

A lightly decorated pattern of sheet music, with petals on the notes. Produced briefly in 1933.

### "FOOTBALL"

Overlapping geometric shapes in yellow, purple, orange, and green, with a blue net. 1929 and 1930.

### FOREST GLEN

A green hillside with a cottage in the middle distance, under a sky painted in the runnings technique of *Delecia* ware, in deep red and gray. Sold in quite large quantities over a short period of time in 1936 and 1937. Newport pattern number 6614. For alternate colorway, see *Newlyn*.

### FOREST LEAVES

Large natural leaves covering most of the ware, painted freehand, no outline. Probably 1932.

### FRAGRANCE

A country garden with tall delphiniums and a large tree, all produced using the etching technique. This colorway, produced briefly in 1935, has small blue and pink flowers in the foreground. Alternate colorway was called *Sandon*.

### FRUIT

An early *Fantasque* design of purple diagonal lines with geometric fruit in red, yellow, orange, and green. Produced briefly in 1930.

### "FRUIT BURST"

A motif of stylized fruit, with orange lines radiating out from behind. 1929 or 1930.

### FUSCHIA

A Newport pottery pattern dating from before *Bizarre* ware, still in production in the early 1930s. Produced on tableware, this would have been painted by the *Bizarre* girls, possibly with either a Newport mark or a *Bizarre* mark. Two colorways, red and blue.

## G

### GALLION

Probably a tableware pattern, design unknown, produced in 1936.

### GARDENIA

A floral design, with half a large flower with salver-shaped petals, two smaller blue and purple flowers, and green and black leaves. When the large flower is red the banding is green; when it is orange, the banding is yellow. A good seller in 1931 and 1932.

### GAYDAY

The same banding as *Crocus*, but with red, purple, and orange asters. Introduced in 1930, and a very good seller through 1934. Alternate colorway called *Sungay*. *Gayday*, like *Crocus*, was produced on a production-line system by painters such as Dorothy Higginson, Edna Cheetham, Winnie Pound, and Elsie Nixon.

### "GEOMETRIC FLOWERS"

A bunch of flowers, each of a different geometric shape, on thin black stems, with diamond-shaped green leaves. A very early *Fantasque* pattern from 1929.

### GIBRALTAR

A seascape with yachts on a blue sea against the Rock of Gibraltar, in pastel pinks, blue, and yellow. Introduced in 1931 and quite a good seller for several years.

### GLORIA

A range produced with a milky glaze, very similar to *Latona*, but with the decoration underglaze. It is very rare, probably produced only very briefly in 1931. Designs used include an adaption of *Crocus*, a tree, and a floral version. All designs painted freehand, no outline.

### GOLDSTONE

A range produced using different clays for the ware. Its speckled finish, as the sales jargon said, showed "minute particles of metal through the glaze." Various shapes including tableware, vases, and wallmasks were produced; all were only lightly decorated to allow the effect to show. Mostly, decoration was of thin wavy lines or freehand flowers. Introduced in 1933, it sold erratically for about eighteen months.

### GORDON

A tableware design, with blue, green, and beige banding, dating from 1935.

### GREEN AURA

An etched shoulder decoration around the rim of pieces of tableware, with the shading across the rim in several shades of green. See also *Yellow Aura*.

### GREEN CHINTZ

The third and rarest colorway of *Chintz*, produced in greens and yellow, with blue detail. Sold in small quantities from June 1932 into 1933. See *Blue Chintz*.

### "GREEN CIRCLE"

An abstract design in green, orange, yellow, and black with circular and castellated shapes. 1929.

### GREEN FIRS

Rare colorway of the *Coral/Blue Firs* design, painted in greens and yellows, only known from one example probably dating from 1934.

### GREEN HOUSE

This early *Fantasque* design is rare, and has a green house with an orange roof, over which is bent a red, green, and yellow tree. The banding is multicolored and the outline is brown. It is the rarer colorway of *Orange House*. Issued late in 1930.

### GREEN JAPAN
See *Blue Japan.*

### GRILL
A tableware pattern with an "L"-shaped motif with stylized flowers around it. Produced in the mid-1930s.

## H

### HARVEST
Ware with a raised motif on its body of wheat sheaves, covered in honeyglaze, with painted details. Introduced in the late 1930s, when it sold well, and also produced briefly after the war. Shapes included tableware, teaware, and decorative jugs.

### HAWTHORN
A lightly decorated tableware pattern produced in blue and orange colorways, with hawthorn leaves and berries. Issued in 1936.

### HELLO
A simple design with spots of various colors over the ware and banding around it. Produced briefly in 1933.

### HOLLYHOCKS
Primarily a tableware pattern in pastel lilac and pink, with beige, yellow, and powder blue banding. It sold sporadically in 1936 and 1937, and was Newport pattern number 6741.

### HOLLYROSE
Stylized flowers with "contour line" pattern between them, produced in an unusual combination of pink, brown, and yellow, briefly in 1932.

### HONEYDEW
A tableware pattern featuring etched flowers similar to the *Rhodanthe* design and partial banding. Alternate version called *Sundew* produced in large quantities in 1935 and 1936. It sold well particularly in the southwest of England.

### HONITON
Shaded bands of color with a pattern formed by dabbing the wet paint with a finger. Clarice named it after the lace town in Devon. Produced by Marjory Higginson sporadically from 1936 onward.

### HONOLULU
A tree with a green-and-black striped stem and pendulous red, orange, and yellow foliage, banded with pale green, overlaid with fine black lines. Sold steadily during 1933 and 1934. Alternate colorway *Rudyard.*

### HOUSE AND BRIDGE
A black-stemmed tree with red, orange, and brown foliage, behind a bridge and a red-roofed cottage by the side of a road. Sold in small quantities but over several years, from late 1931 to 1933.

### HYDRANGEA
Flower heads and leaves in orange, yellow, and brown against thin yellow stripes. Two colorways, orange and green, named after the dominant flower color. 1933.

## I

### IDYLL
See *Applique.*

### INSPIRATION
A range produced by using a combination of metallic oxide

glazes over biscuit ware with the design under the glaze. The ware was decorated in various designs including *Caprice* and *Knight Errant*, plus others with no known names. See also *Persian.*

### ISLANDS
A tableware pattern with a green print of a stylized island, with hand-painted banding. Mid-1930s.

## K

### KANDINA
An abstract pattern of a stylized tree with large oval shapes on either side, below a border of "V" shapes in various colors. Produced briefly in 1929.

### KANG
Ware with raised round shapes covered in a thick gray glaze. Sold in very small quantities in 1935.

### KELVERNE
A tableware pattern with vertical stripes next to leaves and berries, dating from the mid-1930s.

### KENSINGTON
A *Biarritz* dinnerware design of stylized tulips drawn in outline, with geometric hatching through them.

### KEW
Both a tableware and a full pattern with red pagoda, a wedge-shaped tree on one side, and a bubble tree on the other. The full design has on the reverse two orange, poplar-shaped trees and a red bridge. The tableware has the pagoda part of the design, painted in miniature in an oblong on the ware. 1932 and 1933.

### KILLARNEY
Star-shaped geometric design, very similar in form to *Original Bizarre*, but produced in muted shades of green, yellow, and gold. Issued in July 1935, it did not sell.

### KNIGHT ERRANT
An *Inspiration* pattern of a knight on horseback against a stone wall, in shades of blue and brown. Issued late 1931, it sold poorly.

## L

### LATONA
A range with freehand designs painted on a milky-colored glaze. The name was probably an adaption of the word "latex," defined as the milky fluid of a plant. Designs on *Latona* were all exclusive to that ware, and were floral and very colorful. Introduced in 1929 and continued until 1931. The various designs are very similar and difficult to differentiate, but include *Latona Dahlia, Latona Tree,* and *Latona Red Roses.*

### LIBERTY
Produced to bulk-up nonspecific orders. A certain proportion would be supplied covered in a variety of bands, which painters such as Phyllis Tharme painted randomly in any colors and thicknesses they chose. This was much quicker and cheaper to produce than ware that went through the outlining and enameling stages.

### "LIGHTNING"
A 1929 abstract design, which probably was not given a name originally. A black lightning flash crosses a blue and purple disk, and above and below are red, orange, and yellow pyramid shapes. Only produced briefly.

### LILY
Featuring a brashly drawn lily and leaves produced in two colorways: *Lily Orange* (*Fantasque* pattern 104) and *Lily Brown* (107). Both issued in 1929 and only briefly produced before being replaced with more sophisticated designs.

### LIMBERLOST
A brown-stemmed tree with tan foliage and large white flowers in the foreground and a green landscape behind. Sold sporadically 1932.

### LODORE
An early tableware pattern, only partly decorated, with black hatching and a floral motif in green and yellow. 1929.

### LORNA
A landscape with a cottage, a bridge, and a river flowing to the foreground. In natural colors except for some red and orange bushes behind the cottage. Produced briefly in 1936.

### LUPIN
Designed at the same time as *Crocus*, this had the same banding but with tall lupin flowers instead. It is known only from the drawing in the pattern book and one extant example. 1928.

### LUXOR
This early landscape is a mixture of pyramids and pyramid-shaped fir trees. Very rare; 1929 and 1930.

### LYDIAT
Flowers in black outline with pastel green and yellow coloring and amber runnings underneath. 1933.

## M

### MARGUERITE
A variety of shapes produced with raised flowers forming handles or decorative motifs on the ware, the body then mottled in the *Cafe-au-Lait* technique. Flowers painted in either dominant blue or orange. 1932.

### MARIGOLD
A blue glaze with on-glaze decoration of marigolds, painted in naturalistic orange and yellow. Sold poorly in 1931.

### MAY AVENUE
A black-stemmed tree, with green *Cafe-au-Lait* foliage, next to a rising avenue of red-roofed houses and spade-shaped trees. Produced briefly in 1932 and 1933.

### MAY BLOSSOM
Yellow-gray painted ground with black spiky tree with blossoms. Produced in yellow, green, and pink colorways. Very limited production in 1935 and 1936.

### MELON
Stylized fruit with geometric shapes and purple "contour line" effect between. Most common colorway had orange banding, but it was also known in versions with dominant red, green, and pastel shades. 1930 to 1932.

### MILANO
Ware with a mixture of flat surface and light ribbing, with simple bands in one or two colors. May possibly have been an attempt to emulate the style Keith Murray was producing for Wedgwood's at the time, in 1935, but did not sell.

### MODERNE
A tableware range issued in 1929. Ware was banded with platinum-colored lines, with a small oblong in which was paint-

ed the design motif. Each motif had a different name: *Moderne Norge* was two fir trees; *Moderne Odette*, a geometric pattern; *Moderne Paysanne*, stylized flowers. These were sold in sets that included tablecloths and napkins embroidered with the same design motif.

### "MONDRIAN"
An abstract design of overlapping squares very similar to some of the paintings of Mondrian. 1929 or 1930.

### MOONLIGHT
A stylized tree above flowers and leaves on a lined and checkered garden, banded in pastel green and yellow. The same design, in richer colors with orange, red, and black banding, was called *Devon*. Sold reasonably well in 1932 and 1933.

### MOSELLE
Stylized floral design in red, orange, green, and blue, only known from a few examples. Date unknown.

### MOUNTAIN
A rare *Fantasque* landscape with a stylized tree and cottage in the foreground and a tall orange and brown mountain rising up behind. Also referred to in some original literature as *Mountain Cottage*. Rare; only produced briefly in 1931 and 1932.

### MOWCOP
A small tower among trees on a hillock, with a tree in the foreground. Named after a Victorian "folly" at Mowcop in Staffordshire. 1937.

### MR. FISH
Cartoon-type fish swimming amid seaweed. The design mainly seen on sets of hors d'oeuvre dishes. 1936.

### MY GARDEN
A range of ware with handles, knobs, or embellishments of raised flowers. The flowers and body of the ware were available in numerous shades, and four name varieties are known: *My Garden Flame*, with the body covered in deep red and brown runnings; *My Garden Mushroom*, with a matte mushroom-colored glaze; *My Garden Sunrise*, a pale yellow coloring; and *My Garden Verdant*, with a green body. *My Garden* pieces were introduced in 1934 and sold so well that demand for them was just as high two years later. Production continued until the war. Because they are typical of all the ware produced during the 1930s, they are not very collectible.

## N

### NAPOLI
Produced on a mushroom glaze, this was a lightly decorated pattern of a garden with a water fountain under gold stars. Sold briefly in 1937.

### NASTURTIUM
Red, orange, and yellow flowers next to a *Cafe-au-Lait*–style brown mottled area. Pattern sold very well when issued in 1932.

### NEW FLAG
A sophisticated geometric pattern, with V-shapes of various sizes overlapping, forming a complicated multistar design. 1930.

### NEWLYN
The alternate colorway of *Forest Glen*; details identical except the sky is blue. 1935 to 1936.

### NEWPORT
A *Biarritz* tableware design with a combination of banding and

flowers around the shoulder of the plate. 1935.

### NUAGE
Similar in technique to *Cafe-au-Lait*, in that the ware was completely covered with a stippling and then a design was added. *Nuage*, however, seems to have been produced using a thickened paint so that the stippling forms a raised surface on the ware giving it the feel of an orange rind. The designs used with *Nuage* are all large and appear to have been produced with a stencil. Briefly in production in 1931.

## O

### OASIS
A landscape with a large, cloud-shaped, blue tree, with yellow tufts of grass near it. Briefly produced in 1933.

### OPHELIA
On a green glaze, the print of a flower basket with hand-painted flowers in it. Rare but produced both in 1938 and briefly after the war.

### ORANGE AUTUMN
See *Autumn*.

### "ORANGE BATTLE"
One of Clarice's more unusual designs, this resembles one-eyed oranges in conflict amid green stripes, with large drops of perspiration flying off them. Produced briefly in 1930.

### ORANGE CHINTZ
See *Blue Chintz*.

### ORANGE ERIN
A tree shaped like a cloud, in orange with a red edge, and stylized flowers floating around it. An alternate colorway of the design was *Green Erin*, produced in smaller quantities. Both designs date from 1934.

### ORANGE HOUSE
A *Fantasque* design of trees and cottages, this rarer colorway of *Green House* dates from 1930.

### ORANGE ROOF COTTAGE
A cottage by a bridge, with trees and bushes all around, this typifies the landscapes Clarice issued in the early 1930s, and was one of the most popular. Since it was produced over several years, and several of the *Bizarre* girls outlined it, it varies from example to example. This *Fantasque* design appeared in 1932. A rarer colorway is *Pink Roof Cottage*.

### ORANGES & LEMONS
An allover pattern of red, orange, and yellow pieces of fruit with large black leaves between them. Produced in 1931 and 1932.

### ORIGINAL BIZARRE
See *Bizarre*.

## P

### PALM
A stylized palm tree with grass around the base. Produced very briefly in the mid-1930s.

### PASSION FRUIT
A twig heavy with pink and lilac fruit and flowers always seen on a turquoise glaze. A delicately painted design from 1936.

### PASTEL AUTUMN
See *Autumn*.

### PASTEL MELON
See *Melon*. A later colorway issued in 1931.

### PATINA
Biscuit ware randomly splattered with liquid slip in pink or gray and then glazed. This left a surface incrustation that was difficult to paint over. Several simple designs were evolved to be used on this ware. *Patina "Coastal"* had a tree by the edge of a coast; *Patina "Tree"* had a tree with bulbous blue or pink foliage; and *Patina "Country"* was an impressionistic scene with trees and bushes. This ware did not sell particularly well and was complicated to produce, and it was sold only briefly after introduction in August 1932.

### PEBBLES
One of the first *Fantasque* designs, issued in late 1929. A cluster of multicolored circles in repeated panels, between orange and blue bands. Discontinued in 1930.

### PERSIAN (1)
This name was originally given to hand-painted *Isnic* designs issued in late 1928 and 1929. They were produced in brown, greens, and blues and are quite rare.

### PERSIAN (2)
A range produced using *Inspiration* techniques, but featuring Eastern *Isnic*-style patterns in pinks, mauves, and blues. The glazes do not appear to be as thick as the *Inspiration* ones, however. Produced briefly in 1930 and perhaps in 1931.

### PETER PAN
See *Crocus*.

### PETUNIA
Not petunia flowers, but strangely the name given to the alternate colorway of *Canterbury Bells*. Produced briefly in 1934.

### PICCADILLY
A *Biarritz* tableware pattern with a stylized motif similar to *Kensington*. 1935.

### PINE GROVE
Newport pattern 6499, this had boldly drawn black and blue fir trees, the whole design then covered in thin yellow bands. Issued 1935.

### PINK PEARLS
A late 1930s tableware design.

### PINK ROOF COTTAGE
See *Orange Roof Cottage*.

### POPLAR
Named after the two trees, one orange and one blue, next to a cottage on the horizon. In the foreground are large flowers in lilac, blue, and orange. Sold briefly in 1932.

### "PROPELLOR"
Extremely stylized flowers and leaves, the largest flower looking like a ship's propellor, with the contour line effect used on *Melon* between the flowers. Very rare; issued 1931.

### PYRAMIDS
A name used by several of the *Bizarre* girls when referring to the *Original Bizarre* designs, which were based on triangular shapes. These appear to have no individual design names since they were all very similar and were initially colored randomly. Since the name became an unofficial factory reference, however, it is worth noting.

## R

### RAFFIA
A very large range of ware that had surface modeling like woven raffia. Colors were applied to some parts of this, and at least two variations are known from the pattern books—*Raffia Floral* and *Raffia Indiana*. Surprisingly, so large a shape range was produced without test marketing the ware, and it sold badly. Issued in 1936.

### RAINBOW
A tableware pattern with fine banding around the edge of the ware. Most of the banding was in blue and green, but a small part of it changed to red, yellow, and orange. Sold quite well. Issued 1934.

### RAVEL
Issued originally in 1929, this was one of Clarice's most popular tableware designs. Cubist flowers and leaves in jade and orange or red and blue formed a motif on the edge of the ware. Color combinations varied as the design sold first for five or six years and then as matchings.

### RED AUTUMN
See *Autumn*.

### "RED FLOWER"
A flower with geometric leaves and stems running behind and through it. 1930.

### RED ROOFS
A cottage with a climbing plant with orange flowers growing up its wall, in front of a green tree, with a wooden fence on either side. The reverse features a huge orange flower. Issued 1931, only one colorway known.

### RED ROSES
See *Latona*.

### REVERIE
Wavy lines, dot clusters, and a stroke of color made up this later tableware design. 1935.

### RHODANTHE
Took over from *Crocus* in the second half of the 1930s as the factories' best-selling design. Produced by the etching technique, it featured large marigold-type flowers on sinuous brown stems, all on an etched ground with no banding. Issued originally in 1934, it sold until the war, and again after it. Other colorways were *Viscaria* and *Aurea*.

### RUDYARD
The blue and green colorway of *Honolulu*, named after the village of Rudyard, just north of Stoke. 1933 and 1934.

## S

### SANDON
Details same as *Fragrance*, except the flowers are yellow and orange. Named after a village near Stoke. 1935.

### SGRAPHITO
A range of vases with a deeply molded abstract pattern over the whole body of the ware. Produced in various colorings, none of which were successful. Produced briefly in 1930.

### SECRETS
One of Clarice's best-selling landscape designs. A river estuary next to a green hill topped by two brown roofed cottages; on the other side of the bank was a tree with green and yellow foliage. The design, pattern number 6070, was introduced in early 1933 and continued in production for several years, eventually being simplified to a shoulder pattern for tableware. A rarer alternate colorway was produced with brown, orange, and purple shades, and was called *Secrets Orange* after the banding, which was orange.

### "SHARK'S TEETH"
Curved bands of orange, brown, mustard, and yellow with teeth-shaped decoration along the edges. Copied directly from a design by Edouard Benedictus. 1930.

### SILVER BIRCH
A tree with green foliage, a mottled white trunk, and a chocolate and amber colored hill. Unusual in that white was rarely used. Produced briefly in 1937, it appears to utilize a green glaze.

### "SLICED CIRCLE"
A geometric design with radiating lines and circles in orange, yellow, green, and blue, in which some of the circles are on either side of a line. 1929 or 1930.

### "SLICED FRUIT"
A design resembling stylized slices of oranges and lemons. 1930.

### SOLITUDE
An orange and black tree in the foreground, with a red bridge rising from behind it crossing a green, yellow, and gray sea. Plants hang from the bridge. One of the more unusual landscapes, it was produced briefly in 1933.

### SOLOMON'S SEAL
Based on the flower of the same name, this was part of an early experiment to see if it was possible to produce *Bizarre* ware inexpensively by using a printed outline that was then colored by hand. It was not a success, and although it sold for a while, the process was discontinued, as it was deemed to give too regular an outline to the decoration. 1930.

### SPRING CROCUS
See *Crocus*.

### SPRINGTIME
An adaption of the *Crocus* design with orange, red, purple, and yellow crocuses on a green wavy line painted over a green glaze. 1933.

### "STILE AND TREES"
A country stile with trees and bushes on either side of it, produced on a matte glaze. A rare design probably dating from 1937.

### STROUD
A tableware design with brown and amber banding and a small cottage and tree motif. 1933.

### SUMMER
Part of the same range as *Springtime*, this had nasturtiums with a wavy line in blue above and below them on a green glaze. 1933.

### SUMMERHOUSE
This name has been wrongly applied to several of Clarice's designs. It actually refers to the pattern with the red native hut and the green-stemmed tree with yellow cloudlike foliage and pendant red flowers. *Summerhouse* was introduced in 1931 and sold well for two years. No alternate colorway is known.

### "SUNBURST"
Yellow, brown, and orange triangular motif, with a red star shape behind it and orange banding. 1930.

### SUNDEW
The pink and green colorway of *Honeydew*.

### SUNGAY
A variation of *Gayday*, this was actually decorated slightly differently, having a yellow *Cafe-au-Lait* ground, with the asters in yellow, blue, and green. Issued in late 1932.

### SUNGOLD
A later geometric design with yellow and amber, high and low wedges overlapping. 1934.

### SUNRAY
Between stylized skyscrapers, three panels, one with an orange and purple sunburst, another

with a bridge under a star, the third with a deep blue cloud. Produced briefly in late 1929 and 1930.

### SUNRISE

An early *Fantasque* abstract design, with a stylized sunray motif next to wavy lines and clusters of circles. Orange and red colorways. Introduced in late 1929.

### SUNSHINE

Another design produced using a print, this had a brown outline; the flowers were then colored in yellow. Produced briefly in 1930.

### "SWIRLS"

Overlapping curved lines forming a pattern in which each segment is colored differently. 1930.

# T

### TAORMINA

Named after the Mediterranean island, this has a cliff top, a tree in the foreground with etched foliage, and sea and seagulls in the background. Three colorways, but the only variation was the color of the tree. Most common was *Taormina Orange*, then *Taormina Pink*; *Taormina Blue* is also known. Sold quite well, issued in 1936.

### TARTAN

Produced in several colors, a simple tartan pattern used on tableware. 1932 and 1933.

### "TENNIS"

An abstract pattern with purple hatching in the center and straight or curved lines forming the rest of the pattern in blue, gray, yellow, and red. 1931.

### TIBETAN

Although issued with Clarice Cliff marks after 1928, originally a Wilkinson's line produced by John Butler. Luster runnings outlined in gold. Clarice worked on this prior to *Bizarre* ware, applying the gold. Available until 1932, when it was discontinued.

### TRALLEE

One of Clarice's later scenes, produced in the etching technique, it shows a thatched-roof cottage in a country garden. The cottage has shuttered windows, and the *Cafe-au-Lait* style sky is coming out of its chimney. Produced in small quantities in 1935 and 1936.

### "TREE"

One of the first *Fantasque* designs, a very stylized tree with an orange stem and pendulous green and blue foliage. No banding. Very rare; only produced in 1929.

### TREES AND HOUSE

A landscape with a bubble tree, a wedge tree, and a half-hidden cottage. One of the earliest *Fantasque* landscapes, introduced in 1930 initially with dominant red color, but the majority of examples were produced with orange.

The rarest example features the design in seven colors.

### TULIPS

Basically the same garden scene as used in the *Idyll* design, but minus the "crinoline lady." All the elements seem to be taken from Clarice's earlier designs: the black bushes, the tree with hanging flowers, the two poplar trees, and the cottage on the horizon. As with later pieces, however, it was decorated in pastel shades. Issued 1934 and 1935.

### TWIG

A 1936 tableware pattern of a twig forming a small area of decoration on the ware.

# U

### UMBRELLAS AND RAIN

A design with two panels, one with star shapes merging with each other, the second with diagonal lines with colored disks along them. Dominantly green and orange, this was an early *Fantasque* pattern dating from late 1929.

# V

### VIENNA

A tableware pattern with a design of dots and banding dating from 1936.

### VISCARIA

The *Rhodanthe* design in a dominant pink colorway. Issued in

1934, it sold well for several years.

# W

### WHEAT

A print design of ears of wheat with hand-painted color, which was produced briefly on tableware in 1936. Newport pattern number 6485.

### WINDBELLS

A black-stemmed tree, with blue lenticular foliage against a wavy orange, green, and yellow background. Sold in quite large quantities over a short period of time in 1933 and 1934.

### WOODLAND

From behind some blue and purple flowers, a tree with a thin black stem rises to a mass of orange and green foliage. This was Wilkinson pattern number 8869, and it dates from 1931, when it sold briefly.

# Y

### YELLOW AURA

An etched shoulder decoration around the rim of pieces of tableware, with the shading across the rim in shades of yellow and mustard. See also *Green Aura*.

### YUAN

A partial landscape of two cottages and two trees forming a motif on vases, produced on a green glazed background. Very rare. Issued 1937.

Three vases with early designs: "PEBBLES" on a shape 265, FANTASQUE "TREE" on a 269, and "SHARK'S TEETH" on a 265.

## ADDITIONAL DESIGNS

### ACORN

Red acorns amid oak leaves on a tan and yellow *Delecia* ground. Quite rare, produced only in 1934.

### APPLIQUE ETNA

This design can be seen on the charger held by Clarice in the picture on page 42. In the foreground are orange and green trees, in the background a volcano, a blue sea, and black hills. Extremely rare, this design probably never got beyond the sample stage. 1931.

### BRUNELLA

A variation on *Ravel* featuring a very similar design in blue and red. 1929 and 1930.

### CAR & SKYSCRAPER

An example of this design, previously believed to have been only a theoretical drawing, was discovered on an Isis vase in shades of brown, orange, green, and blue. The quality of the piece indicates it was a sample, and the design was never produced commercially. 1932 or 1933.

### CIRCLE TREE

A black-stemmed, spiky tree with rainbow-colored circles as foliage and orange banding. An early *Fantasque* design produced from late 1929 to 1930.

### FLOREAT

A floral design with orange flowers with white centers and green and white leaves on a black ground. 1930.

### FLOWERS & OBLONGS

A design in *Secrets* colorways. Oblongs in green and brown with cubist-style flowers around them. Produced 1932 to 1933.

### ORANGES

Large oranges surrounded by blue, green, and lilac leaves, often seen on a *Cafe-au-Lait* background. A different design from *Oranges & Lemons*, but produced in the same years, 1931 to 1932.

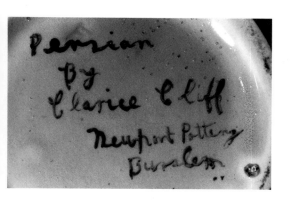

# MARKINGS ON CLARICE CLIFF POTTERY

A mass of marks are to be found on the pottery produced between 1924 and 1941. Although the factory was very fastidious in marking its ware, the quantity and variety of the marks can cause confusion. Once categorized, however, the marks can be used to date a piece of ware accurately. Five different methods of marking were used: hand-painted marks, stamped marks, lithograph marks, impressed date marks, and impressed or raised marks.

## Hand-Painted Marks

When the *Bizarre* name was first introduced it was handwritten on the base of the ware, generally used in conjunction with the "Hand Painted Newport Pottery England" mark already on the ware, underglaze. The handwritten *Bizarre* mark was used from July to October 1928, when it was replaced by the first stamped mark.

As the first *Bizarre* ware appeared Clarice issued *Persian (1)*, the hand-painted *Isnic* design, which had a hand-painted mark. This is extremely rare and dates from September, October, and November 1928. The name was eventually revived for a style of *Inspiration* ware.

*Inspiration* ware appeared in 1929 with a completely handwritten mark. Because the ware went through several firings it was easier to write the mark than use a stamp. The writing is nearly always that of Ellen Browne. Only later, in 1930, was *Inspiration* produced with a stamped mark, with "Inspiration" written above it.

In 1929, 1930, and 1931 hand-painted design names were often used above a standard stamped mark. *Crocus, Latona, Applique, Kandina,* and others were marked this way, but for most cases a custom stamp was eventually made.

From 1931 to 1934 few completely hand-painted marks were used. The factory had an intricate series of lithograph marks during those years, although occasionally hand-painted design names were used above these. Exceptions include the Frank Brangwyn panels and the small advertising plaques designed to stand on dealers' shelves to show alternate colorways and patterns. Because the pieces were so small the mark was generally handwritten. Very few hand-painted marks were used between 1934 and 1941, partly because the factory issued fewer designs during this period.

Throughout the *Bizarre* years hand-painted initials were occasionally included on the ware. A single initial is generally that of the decorator; two initials show that the piece was a sample produced for a particular salesman.

## Stamped Marks

Stamped marks were made by pressing an inked rubber stamp on the ware. Consequently the letters are sometimes smudged, and they also have a rougher outliner than the lithograph marks. The first stamped mark, introduced in October 1928, was the standard "Hand Painted Bizarre by Clarice Cliff Newport Pottery England." This was produced in two sizes and used until 1931. Between 1930 and 1931 a variation on this stamp appeared, with Wilkinson's credited as the manufacturer. Lithograph marks replaced stamped ones in 1931, until 1934, when the "Hand Painted Bizarre by Clarice Cliff, Wilkinson's England" mark from 1930 was revived for one year. Starting at the end of 1935, all the *Bizarre* marks were phased out, and ware was issued with just Clarice Cliff markings. Different versions credited Newport or Wilkinson's as the manufacturer. It would of course have taken quite some time for all the ware with *Bizarre* marks in stock at the shops to be sold, and so no firm date can be determined as to when these marks actually disappeared from the shops.

Stamped marks were also used for many other lines the factory produced. The first *Fantasque* mark with the name in script appeared in late 1929 and was used until the middle of 1930. This was followed with "Fantasque" in capital letters above a standard *Bizarre* mark, which was used until the middle of 1931, when it was replaced by the lithograph *Fantasque* mark.

Customized marks in script style were produced for *Moderne, Latona, Lodore,* and *Delecia* in 1929 and 1930, and marks with the design name in capital letters above a standard *Bizarre* mark are known for *Crocus* and *Gayday* as well as *Fantasque.* These latter marks date from 1930 and 1931.

## Lithograph Marks

Lithograph marks, which replaced the stamped marks in the middle of 1931, were produced in rows on a sheet, cut out, and rubbed onto the bottom of the ware in the same way that actual lithograph designs were transferred to pottery. They can be distinguished from the stamped marks by their finer outline; often it is obvious they were cut from a sheet, as part of the mark is missing or the edge of an adjoining mark is also visible. These were produced in a standard format from 1931 to 1934, with a *Bizarre* mark only crediting Newport Pottery and the range or design name in capital letters above this. The range included marks for *Applique, Cafe-au-Lait, Crocus, Gayday, Delecia, Nasturtium, Nuage, Damask Rose,* and *Fantasque.* Often though, ware was simply given the *Bizarre* part of the mark, regardless of its range or design. Both the stamped and lithographed marks were always applied on-glaze.

## Impressed Date Marks

Date marks are found on ware that was pressed—such as plaques, plates, saucers, and shallow dishes—rather than molded. As a method of stock control the platemakers pressed a die with the month and year on it into the base. The mark was a diamond with two numbers above it: the top one, between 1 and 12, indicated the month; the bottom mark noted the year. Depending on the demand for the ware a piece might have been glazed, decorated, and placed in the shops within two months from the date; at other times it might have remained in the glost warehouse for months or even a year. Therefore these marks only indicate a date before the piece was decorated, not the actual date of decoration.

## Impressed and Raised Marks

The earliest impressed marks are those made by Clarice on the sides of the small figurines she formed from solid lumps of clay. These mainly date from 1924 and 1925, are extremely rare, and represent one of the few examples of ware bearing her name that she actually produced herself.

Many other pieces of Clarice's ware have roughly scratched numbers on them, marks made by the trimmers who joined the pieces of molded ware together before firing. The number was used to assess their productivity and serves no other function.

Much of the molded ware produced has raised or impressed shape numbers on. Numbers in the sequence 14 to 999 indicate the number used by the factory to refer to the shape. The chapter on shapes and shape numbers gives further details on the chronology of these. The numbers 24, 30, 36, and 42 on the base of tea and coffee pots and jugs are not shape numbers but indicate instead the quantity of these pieces that could be fitted into a standard-sized container in the kiln. In other words, the 24 was the largest piece and the 42 was the smallest.

Ware was also sometimes marked with Clarice Cliff's name on the side. This was only rarely done on pieces before 1936, but became more common after that date.

## Wilkinson's Marks

Ware produced for Wilkinson's was fired in the same kilns as those pieces produced for Newport, and throughout the *Bizarre* years Wilkinson's produced honeyglazed pieces with either lithograph or hand-painted decoration. Often Wilkinson's used shapes that Clarice had originally produced for Newport but decorated them much more conservatively. These pieces, which sold alongside *Bizarre* ware in shops, but at cheaper prices, were given one of three markings: the "Honeyglaze" mark ("Wilkinson's England, Honeyglaze Hand Painted"); the "Lion" mark ("Royal Staffordshire Pottery, Wilkinson Ltd, England"); and the "Crown and Shield" mark ("Royal Staffordshire Pottery England, A. J. Wilkinson Ltd, Honeyglaze"). All these marks were underglaze. However, it was often the case, particularly when it was busy, that Newport Pottery ran short of glost ware and used pieces originally intended for Wilkinson's to maintain production. These were given one of the many *Bizarre* marks, although they already had a Wilkinson's mark underglaze. This can cause confusion among collectors, as it has led to the mistaken belief that ware bearing just a Wilkinson's mark was necessarily Clarice's work. And in fact in some cases these pieces are actually of shapes designed by Clarice. Since they were not decorated by the *Bizarre* girls, however, but by the less skilled painters at Wilkinson's, and are in patterns not designed by Clarice, they are not classifiable as Clarice's work. Very occasionally, to confuse matters even further, Wilkinson's blanks decorated in the *Bizarre* shop did not get a *Bizarre* mark on the base, but *are* obviously Clarice Cliff's pottery, as they bear her designs.

The reason the actual *Bizarre* and Clarice Cliff markings were produced with both Newport and Wilkinson's versions was that Newport made such a vast amount of profit after the launch of *Bizarre*, that Colley Shorter credited Wilkinson's with producing some of it, particularly the *Fantasque*, in the early years, in order to spread the tax out. The fact remains that regardless of which factory was credited on the mark, all *Bizarre* and Clarice Cliff pottery produced between 1928 and 1941 was actually decorated in the shops at Newport Pottery.

## Miscellaneous Marks

Many of Clarice's shapes were registered to stop competitors from copying them; therefore pieces were often marked "Registration Applied For" or "Registration No." Since these were applied underglaze, pieces produced after a design was registered still often have "Registration Applied For" marks.

Some companies had exclusive rights to designs produced for them and so the factory added custom marks to the standard marks put on the ware. These include Harrod's, Lawley's, and Brice Rogers Cottage Pottery.

## Classification of Marks

The classification below distinguishes between the *Bizarre*, *Fantasque*, and Clarice Cliff marks and gives a coding that will prove useful to collectors. A further selection of marks is then dated. It is impossible to include examples of all the marks produced, and no attempt has been made to classify the marks produced after World War II.

Misc 1

Misc 2

B5

B3

B2

B1

Script

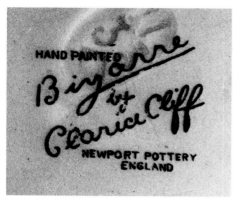

**B4**

## Bizarre Marks

**B1**
The original hand-painted *Bizarre* mark used between July and October 1928. This is nearly always seen with the Newport Pottery stamp, which was on the old stock Clarice used up.

**B2**
The first *Bizarre* stamp mark, produced in two sizes and used between October 1928 and the middle of 1931. It was also produced briefly in gilt in the autumn of 1929.

**B3**
The *Bizarre* stamp mark crediting Wilkinson's, used between 1930 and 1931 and reintroduced between 1934 and 1935.

**B4**
The lithograph *Bizarre* mark only produced with a Newport version. This was used from 1931 to 1934.

**B5**
The lithograph *Bizarre* mark with the *Applique* range credited, as described in the section on lithograph marks above. These marks were used for all or part of the period 1931 to 1934.

## Fantasque Marks

**F1**
The first *Fantasque* stamp mark, produced in two sizes and used between 1929 and 1930. It was also produced briefly in gilt in the autumn of 1929.

**F2**
The second *Fantasque* mark, issued when *Bizarre* became the overall name of Clarice's wares. This appeared in the middle of 1930 and was used until the middle of 1931.

**F3**
The lithograph *Fantasque* mark used from the middle of 1931 until the name itself was discarded in 1934.

## Fantasque Changeover Mark

For a very short period between the *F1* and *F2* marks the *F1* mark was adapted to indicate it was part of the *Bizarre* range by the addition of the *Bizarre* name stamped above it. This mark was used very briefly in the middle of 1930.

## Clarice Cliff Marks

**CC1**
A handmade impressed "Clarice C." mark, this one from the side of a figurine, including the date of production. These pieces were produced by Clarice at Wilkinson's and have a Wilkinson mark on the base.

**CC2**
The standard Clarice Cliff Mark used on nearly all ware issued after *Bizarre* and *Fantasque* were discontinued. Introduced in 1936 and used in various forms with both Wilkinson's and Newport credited until 1941, and from then on with only Wilkinson's credited. However, earlier pieces with small base areas sometimes had the "Clarice Cliff" part of a larger mark on them as they were not big enough to take the whole mark.

## Hand-Painted Marks

A completely hand-painted mark for the *Persian* bowl previously illustrated. This mark was only produced in September, October, and November 1928.
A typical *Inspiration* mark, in Ellen Browne's writing dating from either 1929 or 1930.
The mark from the reverse of the *Blue Firs* advertising plaque previously pictured. These were only produced after 1934, in very small quantities.

## Other "Script" Marks

Examples of designs or ranges that had a custom "script" mark not using the word *Bizarre*. These were produced between 1929 and 1930. Both are quite rare, and in the case of *Moderne*, the actual design name is above the script mark.

## Handwritten Design or Range Names above a Stamped Mark

These are reasonably common, and by ascertaining the date of the mark one can use them to date and name a particular design. The *Applique* example dates from before 1931, as does the *Archaic* one.

## Biarritz Marks

These were applied underglaze to all shapes produced in this range and were used by both Newport and Wilkinson's. Pieces decorated in the *Bizarre* shop had either a Clarice Cliff or a *Bizarre* mark added to them.

**F2**

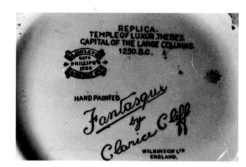

**F1**

**F3**

**FCM**

**Handwritten**

**CC1**

**CC2**

**Script**

**Handwritten**

## SELECTED BIBLIOGRAPHY

The main source of much of the material on Clarice Cliff, Colley Shorter, A. J. Wilkinson's, and the Newport Pottery is the archives of the Stoke-on-Trent Reference Library, and thanks are due the staff for making its services available on numerous occasions.

### BOOKS

Martin Battersby. *The Decorative Thirties*. London: Studio Vista, 1969.
Phillipe Garner, ed. *Phaidon Encyclopedia of Decorative Art*. London: 1980.
William Harvey. *Shelley Potteries*. London: Barrie & Jenkins, 1980.
Peter Wentworth-Shields and Kay Johnson. *Clarice Cliff*. London: L'Odeon, 1976.

### CATALOGUES

*British Art and Design before the War*. Arts Council of Great Britain, 1979.
*Clarice Cliff*. Brighton Museum and Art Gallery, 1972.
*Christie's*. St. James's, London.
*Mobilier et Décoration*. Paris: Editions Edmund Honor, 1929, 1930.
*The Shorter Collection*. Stoke-on-Trent: Louis Taylor & Sons, 1973.
*Sotheby's*. Belgravia, London.
*The World of Art Deco*. Minneapolis, Minn.: Minneapolis Institute of Arts, 1971.

## Photograph Credits

Major artistic color photography by Murray Alcosser

Most black-and-white pictures of collectors' pottery and some original material were taken by Leonard Griffin. Archival photographs of the *Bizarre* girls were loaned by the women themselves. Other black-and-white original material is from the archive at Stoke-on-Trent Library.

The *Nautilus* shape teaware picture is courtesy of Mr. Dave Freeman; the *Butterfly Conical* jug courtesy of Castle Antiques, Warwick; and the Hilda Grindley dedicated plate courtesy of Mr. Eric Grindley.

The English colorplates feature ware from the collections of David and Pauline Latham, Steve and Razia Daniels, Mrs. Betty Scott, Michael Slaney, and Leonard Griffin, and were photographed by Steve Daniels. The American colorplates were photographed by Murray Alcosser and feature ware from the collection of Louis K. and Susan Pear Meisel.

It proved impossible to trace the photographers of some of the original photographs, so unfortunately this can be their only credit.

Project Director: Margaret L. Kaplan

Editor: Beverly Fazio

Assistant Editor: Melvin Shecter

Designer: Carol Robson

First published in Great Britain in 1988 by Thames and Hudson Ltd., London

Reprinted 1989

Copyright © 1988 Louis K. Meisel

Printed and bound in Japan

## INDEX